I0598665

# Snow

Fiction by Ellis Michaels

A Different Kind of Magic

Bad Unicorn

Ordinary Hero

The Bloodfeast Trilogy


Non-Fiction by Ellis Michaels

Finding Happiness Through Pain and
Embarrassment: My Life With Behcet's Disease –
A Memoir


Ellis Michaels Website

ellismichaels.com

# Snow

by **Ellis Michaels**

Infinite Summer Publishing, LLC

ALL CHARACTERS APPEARING IN THIS WORK ARE FICTITIOUS.
ANY RESEMBLANCE TO REAL PERSONS, LIVING OR DEAD, IS
PURELY COINCIDENTAL. ALL RIGHTS RESERVED. NO PART OF
THIS PUBLICATION MAY BE REPRODUCED IN ANY FORM OR BY
ANY MEANS, INCLUDING SCANNING, PHOTOCOPYING, DIGITAL
COPYING, OR OTHERWISE WITHOUT PRIOR WRITTEN
PERMISSION OF THE COPYRIGHT HOLDER.

COPYRIGHT 2021 © ELLIS MICHAELS

FIRST INFINITE SUMMER PUBLISHING EDITION
JUNE 2021

ISBN: 978-1-7333240-7-6

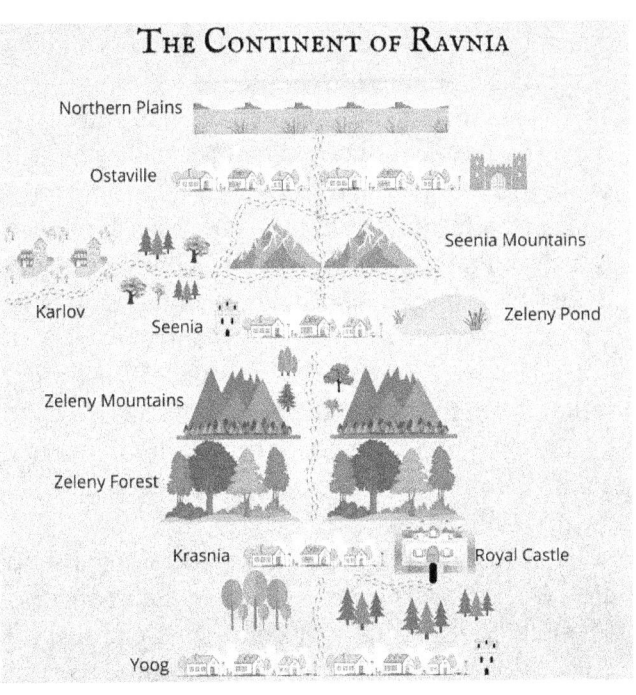

1.

On an unusually cold night, a single snowflake fell from the sky. It was, of course, unique – but not only because it was a snowflake. It was unique because it was the *first* snowflake.

No one had ever seen snow before. Texts from all around the continent going back a dozen generations only spoke of warm summers and cool winters - never hot, never cold.

At first, a single snowflake fell from the sky. It ever-so-gently fell to the ground, melting on contact. Soon a second snowflake fell, followed by a third and a forth. Before long, the skies above the Northern Plains were filled with snowflakes. In the town of Krasnia several-hundred miles to the south, the local tavern was filled with chatter.

"I'm telling you," Rhys said. "White rain is falling from the sky in the Northern Plains."

"Uh huh," Wynn replied. "Sure it is. This coming from the guy who thinks the world was created with magic."

"Think about it," Rhys said, taking a sip of his ale. "Magic keeps getting stronger and stronger. Eventually, it's going to become so strong that a powerful-enough wizard can create entire worlds. How do we know it hasn't already happened? How do we know that some wizard from a world more advanced than ours didn't create *this* world?"

"Because," Wynn replied after taking a long swig of ale, "the whole idea is absurd. We're not living in some sort of magically-created world. Everybody knows the world was created by Xamos. Just like everyone knows white rain doesn't fall from the sky."

"I'm telling you," Rhys said, sitting up straight. "I've been hearing things around Krasnia. People are saying frozen, white rain is falling from the sky way up north. They're calling it *snow*."

"You know what I've been hearing around town?" Wynn asked.

"What?" Rhys replied, taking the bait.

*Buuuuuuuuurrrrrrp!*

The front door swung open and the entire tavern fell silent. In walked the royal messenger, accompanied by two guards. He stopped in the doorway for a moment to look around the tavern. When he spotted Rhys and Wynn, the messenger headed straight for their table.

"Rhys Broadback and Wynn, um-" the messenger read from a small piece of parchment.

"Just Wynn. No surname," Wynn said.

A few patrons gasped.

*I can't believe Wynn just interrupted the royal messenger*, Rhys thought.

"Of course," the messenger continued. "Rhys Broadback and Wynn, you've been summoned to the royal castle by His Royal Majesty and Her Royal Highness at once. Give this to the guards when you get to the drawbridge."

The messenger dropped the parchment on the table. Then, just as abruptly as the royal messenger had entered the tavern, he and the two guards left. The room filled with chatter, twice as loud as before.

"The king, huh?" Wynn said, casually taking a swig of ale. "I wonder what that asshole wants."

"Come on," Rhys shouted. "We have to go."

"After I finish my ale."

"You heard him. *At once* he said."

Wynn chugged the rest of his ale, slammed the mug on the table, and said, "Finished."

The two lifelong friends left the tavern and walked through their hometown of Krasnia toward the royal castle to the east. Though both Rhys and Wynn were human, the town was filled with elves, dwarves, halflings, half-elves, and even a few half-orcs. Wynn strolled calmly down the main road with Rhys several steps ahead of him.

*I can't believe I'm being summoned by the king and queen. What could they possibly want with a couple of young adventurers? Oh, no. Did I do something wrong? Maybe Wynn did something wrong we're both being punished for. That's more likely.*

By the time they got to the royal castle, sweat covered Rhys' entire body. The drawbridge was down with two guards standing in front of it. Rhys handed the parchment from the royal messenger to one of them – the illiterate one – who then handed it to the other. The guard held the sweat-coated parchment by its corner as he read it.

"You may enter," the guard said and stepped aside. The other did the same. "Follow the red carpet. It will take you to the throne room where the king and queen await your arrival."

Wynn walked past the guards and into the castle before they finished speaking. Rhys waited until they were done, nodded to each guard, and hurried after his friend.

*I can't believe I'm in the royal castle. I just hope I'll eventually be able to leave. How many stories have I heard about people getting summoned, never to be heard from again?*

Rhys, once again ahead of Wynn, followed the red carpet deep into the castle. They passed through several doors, each with at least one guard in front of it. Finally, the friends got to the throne room. Rhys knew they'd arrived because he'd never seen such massive doors in all of his twenty-two years. In front of them were two of the biggest guards he'd ever seen. Both grunted as they pulled open the doors.

Rhys and Wynn entered the throne room. It was easily the largest room either of them had ever been in. Rhys was awestruck by the massive tapestries hanging from the ceiling, the jewel-encrusted swords and shields hanging on the walls, masterfully carved statues along both sides of the red carpet, and by the sheer size of the place – not to mention being in the presence of the king and queen. The two friends glanced at each other with raised eyebrows as they followed the red carpet to the far side of the room.

"Kneel before thy king and queen," one of several guards in the room instructed them. There were also a number of servants in there.

The two friends knelt in front of the king and queen in their large, jewel-encrusted thrones – but they weren't the only ones. Another young man as well as a young, female elf were also on their knees in front of the king and queen.

*What are Ena and Malaric doing here? Did one of them do something wrong we're all being punished for? Doubtful. It's probably Wynn.*

The male human and female elf both looked at Rhys and Wynn as they joined them in front of the thrones. Though they weren't all friends – not exactly – they *did* know each other. The four of them had been on several adventures together. Rhys shot Ena and Malaric a what-are-we-doing-here look. Both of them shrugged their shoulders.

The king clapped his hands twice, the sound echoing around the room. The servants and guards stopped what they were doing immediately and turned to face the throne.

"All of you exit at once," the king said. "I need to speak to these four adventurers in private."

"Ahem," the queen coughed, clearing her throat while giving her husband the evil eye.

"*We* need to speak to them," the king corrected.

The queen flashed a half-smile at the king before looking away. All the guards and servants exited the room leaving the four adventurers alone with the king and queen. Rhys' heart thumped so hard he could feel it in his forehead.

"You're probably wondering why I-"

"Why *we*," the queen interrupted.

"Why *we*," the king corrected, *"summoned* the four of you here this morning."

*If it's to kill us, please let it be a quick death. Please, Xamos, let our deaths be swift and painless.*

All four of them nodded.

"*We*," the king continued, glancing over at his wife, "have a quest for you. Will you accept a quest on behalf of the queen and myself?"

"Of course, Your Majesty," Rhys answered.

"It would be an honor," Malaric stated.

"Yes, Your Highness," Ena replied.

"Sure," Wynn said. "Why not."

"Excellent," the queen replied. "The king and I *equally* agreed that the four of you are the right adventurers for this particular quest."

*I can't believe you even know who we are, let alone want us to go on a quest for you. I guess we're not being punished after all. Thank Xamos.*

"Are you familiar with the word *snow*?" the king asked.

"Yes!" Rhys blurted out, his heart nearly beating out of his chest. The others just nodded.

"Good," the queen replied. "We want you to travel north, first to the small town of Seenia, then to Ostaville. Find out all you can about this snow and then report back to us."

"*We* need to know," the king continued, "first and foremost, if snow is real. I have my doubts that cold, white rain is falling from the sky but the queen believes otherwise. If at all possible, lay your own eyes upon this so-called snow. If not, try to talk to people who have seen it themselves. So far we've only heard about it from people who've heard about it from other people. And that simply won't do."

"If you *do* establish that snow is real as I suspect it is," the queen said, "we want to know what's causing it."

"And more to the point," the king added, "if it's any threat to our kingdom."

"Though the king is skeptical about the existence of snow, we're both concerned. And even he can't deny that the air's been cooler than usual. In all the years I've known my husband, I've never seen him wear anything heavier than a light robe – not until these past few months, that is. Lately, we've both required more clothing."

"It's undeniable," the king said. "And no one here in Krasnia seems to have any idea what's been causing the air to cool. We've talked to wizards, alchemists, scholars, monks, and rogues. No one can tell us anything. We've summoned conjurers. We conjured summoners. No one in Krasnia has even the slightest idea why the air is changing. But we suspect the answer may lie to the north."

"And that's where you come in," the queen said. "Travel to Ostaville and back learning all you can along the way."

"I know I can-"

"Ahem!"

"*We* know *we* can count on you," the king said. "Are there any questions about this most important quest you're about to embark on? Now is the time to speak if you wish to do so."

The four kneeling adventurers looked to one another. They all had the same thought which Rhys eventually vocalized.

"I have just one question," he said, his voice shaky. "Traveling all the way to Ostaville and back will require more supplies than any of us can afford. What are-"

"All of your expenses will be taken care of," the queen interrupted. "You'll be given all new gear and supplies. Is there anything else?"

Again, the four adventurers looked at each other.

"No, Your Highness," Rhys replied.

"Excellent," the king said. "You'll leave for Ostaville in one day's time."

The king clapped his hands again and the throne room quickly filled back up with servants and guards. The same guard who'd ordered the four adventurers to kneel returned to his previous spot to order them around some more.

"One at a time," the guard said, "rise to your feet, approach the king, kiss the top of his scepter, and exit the room the same way you came in."

"Ahem!!!"

"Forgive me, Your Highness," the guard said to the queen, bowed, then turned back to the adventurers. "Kiss the scepters of the king *and* queen. Then follow the red carpet out of the castle."

They all did. None of them uttered even a syllable as they exited the castle. All four adventurers were in shock, though Rhys was the only one to have an ear-to-ear grin on his face. Once out of the castle and back in Krasnia, the group finally broke their silence.

"I can't believe we're being sent on an official quest for His and Her Royal Majesty," Rhys said.

"Yeah, about that," Ena replied. "Why *are* we being sent?"

"You heard the king and queen," Rhys answered. "We're being sent to find out if snow-"

"No, I mean why are *we* being sent?" Ena corrected.

"What do you mean?" Rhys asked.

"I'll admit," Wynn said. "I *am* a beast with a warhammer. But Krasnia is filled with more experienced adventurers than us. Why did they pick *us* for this quest?"

"I don't know and I don't care," Rhys replied. "We're going on an official quest for the crown. I may even get to see snow with my own two eyes!"

"And think of all the exotic monsters I'll get to smash between the eyes," Wynn said.

"We've got a lot to do before we depart tomorrow," Rhys said. "Why don't we all agree to meet up at Malaric's at high noon. He lives farther north than any of us close to the road that will take us into the Zeleny Forest. Is that alright, Mal?"

Malaric glanced at Wynn for a second but he didn't notice, then turned to Rhys and replied, "That's fine – I guess."

2.

It was the next day and Malaric expected the others to arrive anytime. He grabbed a couple scrolls from a table in his living room and walked out to the road. In front of a handful of homes – those of Krasnia's literate residents – sat a small wooden box on top of a post just large enough to fit a few scrolls in it. Twice a day, a worker from the town chancery went around to pick up and drop off scrolls from the boxes. And once a week, scrolls were delivered to and from the towns to the north and south of Krasnia.

Malaric put the two scrolls in the box and walked back toward his house. Just before getting to the front door, he saw someone coming up the road.

"You've got to be kidding me," Malaric said under his breath and sighed. But when he realized it was Rhys, Wynn, and Ena, his mood quickly changed. "Oh good. It's just them."

The four adventurers assembled at Malaric's as planned. They waited in Malaric's front yard for the king and queen's men to bring them the equipment they'd been promised.

*Clip, clop, clip, clop, clip, clop.*

"That must be the king's men," Wynn said.

Malaric raised a hand above his eyes to block out the sun so he could see who was coming up the road. He recognized the gallop pattern and knew it didn't belong to any of the king and queen's horses.

"Oh no," Malaric said. "Not again."

A horse came speeding up the road with a single rider on its back. That rider was a teenage boy who lived on the other side of town. He was wearing nothing but a pair of tattered breeches and a full-plate helmet. With one hand on the reins, in the other was a long jousting stick. Malaric already knew what the young man was planning on doing with it as soon as he saw him coming.

*Smash!!!*

Malaric watched his wooden scrollbox shatter into a million pieces. *Scrollbox Jousting,* as it was called, had become a favorite activity among Krasnia's delinquent teens. The sport, if you could call it that, became popular almost immediately after scrollboxes started being used.

"Woo hoo!" the rider yelled as he and his horse disappeared down the road.

Wynn began laughing like a maniac. Malaric slowly walked out to where his scrollbox had been just a minute earlier. He picked his two mangled scrolls from the ground, then began picking up wood fragments. Rhys and Ena went over to help him. Wynn just kept laughing, barely able to stand up straight.

*I hate this town*, Malaric thought while on his knees, picking up pieces of wood. *I can't wait to get out of here. Too bad Wynn has to come with us. He's part of the reason I hate Krasnia.*

Between the three of them, it didn't take long to pick up all the pieces of Malaric's scrollbox – the bigger ones, anyway. By the time they finished, Wynn's laughter had finally stopped.

*Clip, clop, clipidy, clop. Clip, clop, clipidy, clop.*

Again, they heard someone coming up the road. This time it *was* the royal messenger along with two guards, all of them on horseback. The guards' horses each pulled a wagon which the adventurers soon found out was filled with the equipment promised to them. The royal messenger read from a scroll while the two guards handed everything out, one person at a time.

"And lastly, for Wynn: one pack filled with the same items everyone else got, one full suit of heavy chainmail armor, one large pouch with the same amount of platinum, gold, silver, and copper as everyone else, and one brand-new warhammer."

"Look at this freakin' thing!" Wynn yelled, spinning his new warhammer in the air and catching it. Everyone took a step back from him.

"Now that you've received your new equipment," the royal messenger said, "you're to depart at once. His and Her Royal Majesty wish you a successful quest and a safe, speedy return. They want you to know you'll be in their prayers to Xamos every night until you get back to Krasnia."

The messenger motioned for the guards to follow him and they galloped off down the road. All four adventurers examined their new gear, eager to begin their first quest for the king and queen of Ravnia.

"I guess I'll have to mail these scrolls when we get back," Malaric said, returning them to the house his parents had left him when they passed away. He locked the front door and returned to the group. "Are we ready to depart?"

"Been ready," Wynn replied. "We're waiting for you."

"Alright then," Rhys said. "Let's go!"

They headed north up the main road out of Krasnia and into the Zeleny Forest. All of them had spent plenty of time adventuring in the forest, slaying goblins, kobolds, imps, orcs, and other monsters. But most monsters stayed deep in the woods, far away from the main road frequented by traders and travelers. The adventurers stuck to the road and the first few days of their quest went by uneventfully. They did, however, stop to talk to some of the merchants and other travelers they passed along the way. Rhys usually did most of the talking, eager to see if any of them had heard anything about snow. Only one traveler, an elven merchant on his way to Krasnia with a muscular dwarf along for security, claimed to have heard about it.

"Oh, yes!" Halflar, the elven merchant, said. "There's plenty of talk up north about those things."

Halflar's voice was filled with enthusiasm. He was an experienced salesman and could read people like a book. The short, lean elf was able to tell by Rhys' tone that he was dying for someone to talk to him about snow. Halflar was happy to be that person – but not for free.

"Really?" Rhys replied, his eyes wide. "What have you heard?"

"Oh, a little of this, a little of that," Halflar answered. "Speaking of up north, have *you* heard about the high-quality candles that are made all the way up in Ostaville? They're incredibly easy to light and burn for twice as long as regular candles." Halflar turned to the dwarf he was with and said, "Gralol, show these good people one of the candles I acquired up in Ostaville."

Gralol was about the same height as Halflar but nearly twice as wide. The muscular dwarf was a battle-hardened fighter. Gralol had a battle axe strapped to his back, nearly as tall as him. He needed his hands free so he could pull the two-wheeled cart that was filled with all of Halflar's goods. The clever merchant was able to get two jobs done for the price of one. He paid Gralol to not only provide security for him, but also to pull the heavy cart of goods Halflar brought with him from town to town.

The dwarf dug through a number of items in the covered cart, then turned around with a dark-blue candle in his hand. He gave it to Halflar, who passed it to Rhys.

"It's very nice, but I wasn't looking to buy anything today," Rhys said. "I really don't need any more candles."

"I'm sorry to hear that," Halflar replied, taking the candle back from Rhys and handing it to Gralol. "Safe travels."

"Wait a minute!" Rhys said. "What have you heard about snow?"

"You seem nice, but I'm not looking to talk about such things today," the merchant replied.

Rhys' face turned red. He thought Halflar was just being rude. But after getting a look from Wynn, he finally caught on to what the elven merchant was trying to do.

"On second thought, maybe I am looking to buy a new candle," Rhys said.

"Maybe I'm looking to talk about snow," Halflar replied.

The two of them haggled for a minute, something Rhys wasn't particularly good at. He ended up buying two candles, paying more than twice what he would've paid for a couple of candles back in Krasnia. It got the merchant to talk though, so Rhys was happy. Wynn shook his head as he watched his friend overpay.

"Well?" Rhys asked.

"I was in Ostaville not too long ago," Halflar replied. "As I'm sure you know, Ostaville is the last towns before you get to the Northern Plains. I met several people there who claim to have seen hard, white rain falling from the sky. As you seem to already be aware, they're calling it *snow*. Though only a handful of people claim to have actually seen it, most of the town believe it's real. In fact, if you *don't* believe it, they call you a *snow denier* and ridicule you. That's how prevalent the idea is becoming up there."

"See?" Rhys exclaimed, looking right at Wynn. "I told you snow is real!"

"I'll believe it when I see it," his friend replied. "I'm not taking some random merchant's word for it and neither should you."

"Thank you so much," Rhys said, returning his attention to Halflar. "I'll let you be on your way."

"And thank you for your business. I think you'll find they're the best candles you've ever used."

"Will you give him a money-back guarantee?" Wynn asked.

"Oh, they'll be the best candles he ever uses," Halflar replied to Wynn, then looked at Rhys. "But, in case I haven't mentioned it already-"

"Let me guess," Wynn interrupted. "All sales are final?"

Smiling, Halflar replied, "You took the words right out of my mouth. All sales are final. Safe travels."

The group continued north through the Zeleny Forest. By their fourth day of travel, Rhys and Wynn were father north than they'd ever been. Ena and Malaric had both been as far north as Seenia. It's where Ena was born, though her family moved to Krasnia when she was a child. The farther north they got, the more mountainous the terrain became. On both sides of the main road, which stayed at the same elevation, were massive mountain ranges covered in trees.

*Zip!*

"Did you just hear that?" Wynn asked, stopping in the middle of the road.

"Hear what?" Rhys asked.

"It sounded like something just whipped right past my head."

"I didn't hear anything," Malaric replied.

*Zip!*

"I just heard it, too," Ena said.

*Zip!*

Zip, zip!

Zip!

Zip, zip, zip!

"Arrows," Wynn yelled. "Take cover!"

Both sides of the road were densely filled with trees making it hard to tell where the arrows were coming from. Rhys was the only one with a shield and raised it up to protect his face. As soon as he did, an arrow came zipping through the air and stuck right into the middle of the wooden shield.

"They're coming from over there!" Rhys yelled, pointing left of the road.

They all ran into the woods, each taking cover behind a tree. Ena pulled a book out and started reading the words to a spell. Pinned down by oncoming arrows, the others stayed put where they were. Both Rhys and Wynn bravely peeked out from behind the safety of their trees, trying to get an idea of who and how many they were up against.

"Goblins!" Wynn yelled, briefly catching a glimpse of one as he poked his head out from behind the tree.

"How many?" Rhys asked.

"No clue," Wynn replied. "More than one, for sure."

*Zip!*

Zip, zip, zip!

Zip, zip!

Malaric could see Wynn from where he was standing. Wynn wrapped his hands tightly around the handle of his warhammer and raised it up.

*He's actually going to do it. That crazy fool is going to charge into a bunch of incoming arrows.*

"Die!" Wynn yelled as he left the safety of his tree and charged at the goblin he'd spotted.

The green monster grabbed an arrow from his quiver, lined it up, pulled back the string of his short bow, and took aim at Wynn's face. But a split second before letting the arrow fly, the head of Wynn's warhammer met the goblin's face.

*Crunch!*

The blow instantly killed the goblin and its body fell to the ground. An arrow whizzed past Wynn's head as he rushed back to once again hide behind the same tree.

Ena came to the end of her spell, one of the only multi-target spells she knew that didn't require being able to actually see the targets. Facing the direction the arrows were coming from, the dark-skinned elf raised one of her hands while holding her book in the other and read the final words to the spell.

"Cover your ears!" Ena yelled as soon as she finished casting it, then dropped the book and covered her own. "Now!"

Malaric and Rhys followed her instructions.

"Do what?" Wynn asked.

The sky, which had been perfectly clear all day long, suddenly filled up with thick, grey clouds. Several bolts of lightening came slicing down through the air, each one hitting a different goblin. It happened so quickly that all anyone saw was a single bright flash, followed by the deafening sound of thunder.

*Boom!!!*

Everyone stayed perfectly still, listening for incoming arrows. When they didn't hear any, each of them cautiously came out from the tree they were hiding behind. Wynn walked deeper into the forest past the goblin he'd killed until he came upon another one. It was lying on the ground with smoke coming off its corpse. The goblin's fingers were still wrapped around its bow.

"This one's dead!" Wynn yelled.

"Shhh," Rhys replied. "Some of the others might not be."

"What?" Wynn asked, still yelling.

With their weapons in hand, the group cautiously explored the area. They wanted to make sure all the goblins were dead. After a few minutes of searching the woods, everyone was confident Ena's spell had eliminated the threat entirely. They found six goblins in all, five of them with a bow either still in hand or right next to their corpse. One goblin who was clearly their leader, they found with his fingers still wrapped around a dull, rusty shortsword. The others were all wearing tattered clothing. The goblin with the sword wore much nicer clothes, which only had a few rips in them.

"This is strange," Rhys said, standing over the goblin-leader's corpse.

"What range?" Wynn yelled.

"Why are you yelling?" Malaric asked Wynn.

"Why is who telling?" he shouted.

"Wynn's yelling," Ena replied to Malaric, "because he didn't cover his ears like the rest of us did."

"Oh," Malaric replied, trying to hide a smirk. Malaric could've easily reversed the damage done to Wynn's hearing. Though trained to be a rogue by his parents, Malaric decided to switch to the healing arts after they passed away. He could've easily healed Wynn's ears but didn't offer to. Malaric knew Wynn's hearing would recover on its own – eventually.

Everyone gathered around the dead goblin leader Rhys stood over. It didn't take long for the others to pick up on what Rhys was talking about. The goblins that attacked them were no ordinary goblins – they were mountain goblins.

"I've never heard of mountain goblins coming down this far," Ena said. "And certainly not attacking people along the road."

"What do you suppose they're doing down here?" Malaric asked.

"I have no idea," Ena replied.

"I do," Rhys said. Everyone looked at him. "I think I do, anyway. Mountain goblins are used to living up in the mountains."

"No shit," Wynn yelled.

"Hear me out," Rhys said. "They're used to living up in the mountains where the air is cooler. If the continent is getting colder like some people are saying, then what's the first place that'll really feel it?"

"Higher elevations like up in the mountains," Ena answered.

"Exactly," Rhys exclaimed. "And if it gets too cold in the mountains, all the monsters and animals living there will have no choice but to move somewhere more hospitable."

"So you think mountain goblins came all the way down here because it's too cold up in the mountains?" Malaric asked. "I guess that makes sense."

"Makes sense to me," Ena said. "What do you think, Wynn?"

"What?" he shouted.

"Never mind," Ena replied.

They searched the mountain goblins but didn't find anything of value, aside from a couple of copper pieces. The adventurers got back on the road and continued north through the Zeleny Mountains to the small town of Seenia.

3.

*Home sweet home*, Ena thought as they approached a wooden sign on the side of the road that read *Welcome To Seenia* in the common language.

Just a little father up the road stood a much-newer sign Ena had never seen before. Written in four different languages – Common, Elvish, Dwarven, and Halfling – this sign read: *Use of fire magic is strictly prohibited in Seenia and all points north.*

"That's strange," Ena said.

"What?" Rhys replied.

"This sign. It wasn't here the last time I visited Seenia. I know it's been a few years, but it looks like a lot has changed."

"If you don't like the sign, I can bash it down," Wynn offered.

"That's sweet of you," Ena replied. "But please don't bash anything down in my hometown."

"Suit yourself," Wynn replied.

They entered the town of Seenia after five long days of traveling through the Zeleny Forest. It was a small town, about half the size of Krasnia. Wynn took out a gold piece and began flipping it over and over as they headed into town.

"Traveling sure makes me thirsty," Wynn said. "Where's the tavern in this weird-ass town?"

"Seenia's not weird," Ena replied, slightly offended. "I love this town. It's where I was born, you know. Although, now that you mention it... Seenia *has* changed quite a bit from how I remember. Let me give you a tour of the town and then we'll go to a tavern."

The father they got into town, the weirder it

got. In front of several homes were signs that said things like *End Dagger Violence*, *People Don't Kill People – Swords Kill People*, and *Goblinoid Lives Matter*.

"Haha," Wynn chuckled, still flipping the gold coin. "No they don't."

As Wynn flipped the coin for the hundredth time, a man wearing tattered clothing and an eyepatch over his left eye came out of nowhere, snatched the coin mid-air, and bolted down the road.

"Son of a-" Wynn yelled. "Oh no you don't!"

Wynn took off after the thief. For a man wearing heavy chainmail armor, Wynn was surprisingly fast. The thief turned left off the main road and ran through someone's yard. Wynn turned the corner just in time to see the thief climbing over a tall wooden fence. He charged after the man and leapt up grabbing the top of the fence, but couldn't lift himself over it. As strong as Wynn was, between the armor, the warhammer on his back, and the heavy backpack he had on, he couldn't lift himself. But Wynn didn't give up. He tried to ram his way through the wooden fence.

The others rounded the corner of the house just in time to see Wynn run full-speed into it. The fence didn't budge. Wynn went crashing to the ground, slightly dazed.

"Don't laugh," Rhys said to Malaric.

"I wasn't going to," he lied, letting a few chuckles slip out.

"That lousy, good-for-nothing pirate-ass piece of..." Wynn muttered as he stumbled his way back up to his feet.

"Are you alright?" Rhys asked.

"Do I not look alright?" Wynn replied.

*You look like you just ran into a wall*, Ena thought.

"Just making sure you're okay," Rhys said. "Come on. Don't worry about the gold piece. The king and queen gave us all more than enough. Let's keep checking out Seenia."

"I hate this fucking town already," Wynn said as he dusted himself off.

"And I like it already," Malaric said under his breath, just loud enough for Ena – but not Wynn – to hear.

She continued to show them around Seenia. Ena wasn't kidding: a lot *had* changed since the last time she'd been there. Besides signs posted in both public and private places, she noticed a lot of people dressed differently than usual. Shop names had changed, buildings that had been there since she was little were now gone, and several new ones had sprouted up all over town.

"Can we go get some food and drinks now?" Wynn asked. "Or at least some drinks?"

"Soon," Ena replied. "I just want to stop by the black-magic shop first. It's on the way."

*Well, that's strange*, Ena thought when they got there. *Ever since I was a little girl the sign's always said Black Magic Shop. I wonder why they changed it to just Magic Shop. I'll have to ask once I'm inside. The building looks bigger, too. And I wonder what happened to the white-magic shop next door. It looks like it got torn down not too long ago.*

"I'll be out here," Rhys said.

"Me too," Wynn added. "Don't take too long."

"Malaric?" Ena asked. "You going to come in with me?"

"I thought you said it was a black-magic shop?"

"It *was*," Ena replied. "But now I'm not sure. They changed the name. Maybe they sell white-magic supplies now, too."

Malaric agreed to go in with Ena. Once inside, she quickly realized that it wasn't the same black-magic shop she'd been in a half-dozen times before. The old one offered – unsurprisingly – only items related to the dark arts. But this shop also sold supplies related to the healing arts and other types of white magic.

"Welcome to the magic shop," a half-elven man wearing several rings and a multicolored robe said from behind the counter. "Your one-stop shop for all things magic related – everything but fire magic, of course."

"Thank you," Ena replied. "I have a question about that. But first, I have a different question."

The half-elf nodded, smiled, and said, "I'm happy to answer *all* your questions."

"Though my parents moved to Krasnia when I was young, I was born here in Seenia and have been back several times. The last time was a few years ago."

"I'm not sure how to answer that," the half-elf replied, scratching the pointy tip of one of his ears.

"I haven't gotten to a question yet. I was going to say, of all the times I've been in Seenia, this has always been the black-magic shop. And next door has always been the white-magic shop. What happened to the shop next door and why did you change the name of this one?"

The half-elf eyed Ena up and down with contempt, his smile gone. Ena noticed, though she did her best to hide it.

"This *is* still a black-magic shop, isn't it?" Ena asked. "You're a black mage like me, aren't you? You certainly look like a wizard, someone who practices the dark arts."

"I've heard about how behind the times they are in Krasnia," the half-elf finally replied. "So I suppose it's not your fault you don't know any better. Here in Seenia we don't use offensive words like *black* magic or *white* magic."

"Oh," was all Ena could say.

"You're right about one thing, though: I *am* a wizard. But I'm not a bla – I don't even like to say that word. I'm not a B mage like you insinuated."

"I didn't mean to insin-"

"I'm a non-binary wizard," the half-elf interrupted.

"A what?" Malaric asked, finally joining the conversation.

"I practice both B magic *and* W magic, just like every wizard in Seenia and all points north."

"Oh," Ena said again.

"Here's a friendly piece of advice from one wizard to another," the half-elf said to Ena. "While in Seenia – and certainly anywhere north if you're traveling that way – I wouldn't go around calling yourself a B mage. Others aren't as understanding as me."

"Thanks for the advice," Ena replied. *I think.* "And my other question is about the fire-magic ban. When did that happen? And why?"

"Fire magic hasn't been banned in Seenia for very long. A few months at most. But it was banned in Ostaville several months before it got banned here. That's the way things usually happen: they start in Ostaville and work their way down here. They're a very progressive town, you know. Ostaville was the first town to do away with B and W magic long before Seenia did."

"But *why* was fire magic banned?" Malaric asked.

"Do you really have to ask that?" the half-elf scoffed. "Fire magic can be extremely dangerous. Since it was banned in Seenia a few months ago, fire-related deaths have gone way down."

*That's the whole point of fire magic – and black magic in general. It's supposed to be dangerous.*

Each answer spawned more questions Ena wanted to ask, but the confused wizard thought it'd be best to let it go for now. She could tell Malaric was just as curious, be he stayed quiet, too.

"Thank you for answering our questions," Ena said to the half-elven shopkeeper and turned to leave.

"Don't you want to buy anything? The magic shop has all your non-binary magical needs."

"Some other time, maybe," Ena replied.

Her and Malaric left the shop and joined the others outside.

"Jeez," Wynn said. "Finally. *Now* can we go to the tavern?"

"There is no *the* tavern," Ena replied.

"What?" Wynn yelled, his face turning bright red. "There's no tavern in this shitty town?"

"I didn't say that. I said we can't go to *the* tavern because there isn't just one. But we can go to *a* tavern because Seenia has three – or at least they did the last time I came up here."

"Don't do that," Wynn said and took a deep breath. "I was about to whip out my warhammer and start going berserk on this whole town."

"Which tavern do you want to go to?" Ena asked.

"What are our choi-" Malaric started to ask but Wynn cut him off.

"Whichever one is closest."

"Follow me," Ena said.

She led them through the center of town to a nearby tavern not far from the magic shop. It was a large building and in much better condition than Ena remembered it. Above the door to the tavern was a sign that, in the common language, read: *The Scene*. They could tell the place was packed before even getting to the door. Loud chatter, mugs clinking together, and the sound of music being played could all be heard from outside the tavern.

"This looks like my kind of place!" Wynn said, glancing back at Rhys as he opened the door and walked in.

Their ears had not deceived them: the tavern was loaded with patrons. There were only two open tables, the rest filled with men and women of all races, ages, and occupations. In the far corner of the tavern stood a multi-raced woman with the ears of an elf, stature of a dwarf, hairy hands of a halfling, and the voice of an angel singing while playing a lute. Next to her sat a dwarven man beating a small tabor drum with one hand and using the other to blow into a three-holed tabor pipe. In front of them danced several patrons, some of them singing along. Everyone in The Scene seemed to be in a good mood – everyone but Wynn.

"Son of a bitch," Wynn said when he spotted the eyepatch-wearing man who'd stolen his gold piece earlier. The man was sitting at the bar with a half-empty mug in front of him and an ear-to-ear grin plastered across his face.

4.

*I'm going to kill you, you pirate-looking piece of shit*, Wynn thought as he walked right up to the man with the eyepatch. *I'd smash your skull in with my warhammer if there weren't so many people in they way.*

"Wynn, don't do anything that will-" Rhys started saying.

"Too late," Malaric added.

Wynn approached the eyepatch-wearing man from the side, grabbed the legs of his barstool with both hands, and yanked it out from underneath him. The skinny man went flying to the ground, landing on his backside. His half-empty mug of ale went with him spilling all over the place, quickly becoming a fully-empty mug.

The entire tavern fell silent. Even the man and woman playing music in the corner stopped, as did everyone who'd been dancing. All eyes were on Wynn.

"I'm going to kill you," Wynn said, standing over the ale-soaked man.

Wynn made a fist, leaned down, and shook it at the terrified thief. He curled into a ball, holding his hands in front of his face. Four large men, all wearing armor, got up from a table and approached Wynn.

"You'll do nothing of the sort, stranger," one of them said. "Seenia's a peaceful town and The Scene is a peaceful tavern. What's your gripe with Pax?"

"This piece of shit stole a gold piece from me," Wynn replied. "I should make Pirate Pax walk the plank. Swab the deck with his face."

"Pax, is this true?" one of the large, armored men asked.

"I didn't think it would be a big deal," Pax answered from the floor, then sat up. "He's got such fancy armor and equipment, I didn't think he'd miss a mere gold piece."

"You thought wrong," Wynn replied and shook his fist at Pax again even though he was surrounded by armed men.

"Here," the barmaid behind the counter said to Wynn, flicking him a gold piece. "And I'll give you a free mug of ale if you leave Pickpocket Pax alone. We don't want any trouble in here."

"Or out there," Pax added, pointing to the door.

"Don't worry about that," the barmaid said to Pax. "You won't be going out there for a long time. You're going to pay me back for the gold piece and the free ale by working here at The Scene and at my inn next door for a week. From now on you're Porter Pax. And you can start right now by mopping up the ale you spilled everywhere."

"Yes ma'am," Pax replied.

"Free ale and you leave Pax alone in here *and* out there," the barmaid said to Wynn. "Deal?"

"Fine," he replied.

The four adventurers sat down at one of the empty tables and the four large men returned to theirs. Once Pax managed to get back up to his feet, the barmaid gave him a mop and bucket to clean up the ale he'd spilled. She then brought Wynn the free mug he'd been promised. Rhys thanked the barmaid for his friend. Wynn was too busy chugging the tall mug of ale which he finished before she'd even gotten back to the bar. The two musicians resumed playing and the tavern quickly filled with chatter and laughter. A different woman soon came over to the table to take their food and drink orders.

"Welcome to The Scene: Seenia's oldest tavern. What can I get for you four human trav-" The woman paused when Ena pulled down the hood of her cloak. "Excuse me. What can I get for you human-and-elven travelers?"

"I'm not human," Malaric said. "I'm a halfling."

"Oh, here we go," Wynn mumbled under his breath, still loud enough for Malaric, Rhys, Ena, and their server to hear.

"My apologies," the woman corrected. "I shouldn't have assumed you identify as human just because you look human."

"Yes," Wynn replied, "you should have. Because he *is* human."

"You know damn well I identify as a halfling and have for a long time!" Malaric said to Wynn.

"You can identify as a dragon with the hairy feet of a gnome and pointy elf ears, but it doesn't make it true. You're human. Just accept it!"

"Your accent," the server said, looking at Wynn. "Where are you from? Yoog?"

"Yes," Wynn replied, surprised. "I mean no. I'm from Krasnia. But my parents were from Yoog. Good ear."

"Well then, that explains it. Krasnia's not nearly as progressive as Seenia is. And Yoog is even more behind the times. But here in Seenia, we respect each others' identities."

*In Yoog and in Krasnia – for the moment, anyway – we respect each others' actual identities, not whatever they feel like calling themselves at the time,* Wynn thought but didn't say anything.

"In Seenia," the server repeated slower and louder, "we respect each other's identities. In The Scene we respect each other's identities. Do you understand?"

*I understand that you, along with the rest of this town, is crazy.*

Wynn still didn't reply.

"Do. You. Understand?" she asked again.

*The sooner I play along with her silly game, the sooner I can get more ale.*

"Sure, I understand," Wynn reluctantly replied. "Now can I get another ale? And some food?"

This time, *she* didn't reply.

"Please?" Wynn added, taking the hint.

"Of course, darling!" the server replied, her tone going up half an octave. "What'll ya have?"

They all placed their food and drink orders, then the server disappeared behind the counter. The four adventurers began talking among themselves. A conversation happening at the table directly behind them caught Malaric's ear. He turned around to see who they were: three halfling men. As soon as he did, they stopped talking and stared at him.

"Excuse me," Malaric said. "I don't mean to eavesdrop, but did one of you just say you were human before transitioning into a halfling?"

"That's right," one of them replied, pointing to another halfling at their table. "Calum here was. What's it to ya?"

"I'm a human rogue-healer who identifies as a halfling," Malaric said. "Can I ask you a few questions?"

"Sure," Calum answered.

Wynn rolled his eyes. Malaric didn't seem to noticed. Rhys *did* and shook his head.

"I'm thinking about transitioning," Malaric said. "What is the process like?"

"It's not as bad as some people make it out to be," the human-turned-halfling replied. "First, you have to have a transition spell cast on you. Only certain wizards who have been approved are allowed to cast it. That changes your body. Then," Calum said, pulling out a small pouch and tossing it on the table, "you have to take certain herbs to make sure the changes stick. If you don't take them, you slowly revert back to your old race."

"Ugh," Wynn said. "What smells like a foot just ripped a fart?"

"I'll admit, the herbs are a bit pungent," Calum said. "But it's a small price to pay to feel comfortable in my own skin. What other questions do you have?"

"When did you know you were a halfling?" Malaric asked. "And how long ago did you transition?"

"He's always known," one of the others at their table said. All three halflings laughed.

"It's true," Calum agreed. "I have."

"When he was eleven," one of the other halflings said, "he went through a big growth spurt and grew nearly a foot in just a few months. He hated it and wanted to be short like us. So he started walking around on his knees everywhere."

"I remember that," Calum said. "I hated getting so tall. But yeah, to answer your question: I've always know. As long as I can remember, anyway. But I didn't transition until just a year ago. Before then, there weren't any good transition spells that lasted a long time. They're a relatively new thing."

"I've never actually met anyone who has transitioned into a halfling before," Malaric said. "Or transitioned into anything, for that matter. Where we're from, it's not really talked about. In fact, people give me shit for being transracial all the time," Malaric said, glancing over at Wynn. He didn't seem to notice. "Last question: Any regrets? Are you happy you transitioned?"

"This past year has been the best year of my life. After transitioning, I felt normal for the first time. And fortunately, I've got great friends who have always been supportive. I haven't regretted my decision for even a second."

"That's great to hear," Malaric replied. "Thank you. I'll let you three get back to your meal. Thank you very much."

"You're welcome," Calum replied and smiled. "Best of luck."

The server returned with their food and drinks just as Malaric's conversation with the halflings ended. He turned back around and they stuffed their faces. After finishing their meals, they all ordered another round of drinks. Wynn ordered two.

"So, what's next?" Wynn asked Rhys. "As far as I'm concerned, the sooner we get out of this town, the better."

"I'm not in any hurry to leave," Malaric said. "I like it here."

"You *would* like it here," Wynn replied.

"What's that supposed to-"

"How about this," Rhys interrupted. "Why don't we spend one more full day in Seenia. That will give Ena some time to catch up with a few friend and see if they've heard anything about snow. And it'll give us a chance to do some more exploring and asking around as well."

"Sounds perfect," Ena replied.

"Works for me," Malaric said.

"Fine," Wynn replied. "One more day. Then we resume heading north so I can put the head of my warhammer through the heads of new monsters I've never even heard of."

5.

The next morning, the adventurers gathered outside the inn to figure out the plan for the day.

"I have an friend I've known since I lived here as a little girl," Ena said. "She'd be furious if she found out I was in town and didn't come see her. Anyone want to come with? Wynn?"

"Is your friend hot?" he asked.

"Her husband seems to think so."

"Pass," Wynn replied but quickly reconsidered after glancing at Malaric and Rhys. "On second thought, if I go with you, at least I'll get to interact with a woman or two. Women avoid these two as if they were wearing a Ring of Repulsion and an Anti-Attraction Amulet or something."

Ena laughed until she realized Rhys and Malaric were both giving her the evil eye. She promptly stopped.

"Go ahead," Rhys said to Ena and Wynn. "You two go visit your friend. See if she knows anything about snow, the weather getting colder, the fire-magic ban, or anything else out of the ordinary. Malaric and I will explore the town some more, trying to learn as much as *we* can about those things. Then we'll all meet here in the mid-afternoon."

Ena nodded, then disappeared down the road with Wynn. The second they were gone, Malaric turned to Rhys.

"I really can't stand him."

"I know, Mal. He can be-"

"I don't understand how someone like *you* can be friends with someone like *him*."

"I've known Wynn since we were little," Rhys explained. "I was the first friend he made in Krasnia."

"And I'm pretty sure the last. I just don't get why you constantly defend him."

*I don't constantly defend Wynn, do I? Maybe a little bit. But not constantly.*

"He had a difficult childhood," Rhys said. "Wynn's parents aren't from Krasnia like ours. They're from Yoog. And down there, things are a lot different. He's really not as bad as-"

"There you go proving my point," Malaric said. "You're defending him again."

"Forget about Wynn. If you hate him that much, enjoy the few hours away from him we've got. Let's go wander around Seenia."

*And as much as I like Wynn, I can always use a break from him every once in a while myself. The last thing I want is to listen to you talking about Wynn while he's off with Ena.*

Rhys and Malaric walked around the town, talking to a few people they passed along the way. Seenia was a small town with strong community values. The residents discouraged adventuring, which is why Ena's family had moved south to Krasnia. Very few adventurers actually lived in Seenia, though several were passing through at any given time. Between the monster-filled forests directly north and south of the town, and the fact that it was roughly halfway between Krasnia and Ostaville, Seenia was a popular place for adventurers to rest, stock up on supplies, and stuff their faces. While the town didn't want its residents to be adventurers themselves, they had no problem profiting from adventurers visiting from other towns.

At about mid-day, Rhys and Malaric noticed some Seenia residents walking hurriedly toward the town center. Rhys stopped one of them to ask why they were in such a hurry.

"The Prophet is in town," the dwarven woman said.

Both Rhys and Malaric replied with blank stares.

"You know: The Prophet," the dwarf said. "The Prophet of Karlov? Sandor Perjonet?"

"Who's The Prophet of-" Rhys started to ask.

"I'm sorry," the woman said and continued down the road even faster than before, still talking until they could no longer hear her. "I don't want to miss what The Prophet has..."

*Now I don't want to miss what this prophet has to say – whatever it is. Whoever it is.*

Rhys and Malaric glanced at each other. Without saying a word, they both turned and started following the dwarven woman toward the center of town. It didn't take much time for the longer-legged humans to catch up to her.

In Seenia's center, a male human stood over a small-but-growing crowd, standing atop a large wooden box. The dwarven woman weaved her way through the crowd to the front so she could see. Rhys and Malaric, both tall enough to see over most of the crowd, stood toward the back and listened.

"This isn't something to be taken lightly," the frail, well-dressed man said confidently. "This isn't a fairy tale like The Tale of the Fairy's Tail. Snow is real! I've talked to the sharpest minds in Karlov, Ostaville, and even right here in Seenia. They're all in agreement that frozen rain has been falling from the sky up north. And it won't be long before it starts happening here."

Several people in the crowd gasped. Rhys' lips were parted slightly as he eagerly listened to what Sandor had to say.

"Now it may sound harmless: frozen, white rain falling from the sky. And it very well may be. But temperatures are plummeting all around the continent of Ravnia. If it continues to get much colder, we could all be in some real trouble."

"What can we do?" an elderly elven man in the crowd asked.

"What's causing the cold?" a young human woman shouted.

"It all started when fire magic was banned – first in Ostaville and then here in Seenia. It's only been since the beginning of the fire-magic ban that the temperature has been going down. Now as a scholar, I have to remind myself that just because two things happen at the same time doesn't mean they're necessarily connected. There could be other forces at play causing the air to cool and snow to fall from the sky. But I think the most likely explanation is that the fire-magic ban is to blame. Less fire means less heat."

Rhys stared at Sandor Perjonet with admiration. He was much older than Rhys. Sandor had salt-and-pepper hair with a clean-shaven face. He wore a custom-tailored tunic, pants, and jacket, all made from fine fabrics, as well as a pair of matching shoes – both in color and quality. Though Sandor had a thin frame and stood slightly slouched over, his voice was loud and he spoke with both confidence and clarity. And for some reason, the fact that he had a thick Karlovian accent made Sandor sound more credible.

"But there's an even more pressing issue at hand," he continued. "The banning of fire magic is unprecedented. Sure, things have been banned before. That's nothing new. And sometimes bans are a good thing. Like when this very town – you, the wonderful people of Seenia – banned fishing in the pond to the east."

"Zeleny Pond!" a crowd member shouted.

"That's right: Zeleny Pond. When you banned fishing in Zeleny Pond, it was a good thing, right? People stopped dying from eating the poisonous fish that live in the pond."

"The three-eyed Carrot Fish!" someone in the crowd yelled. Sandor didn't respond. He just kept talking.

"Sometimes – like in this case – bans can be a good thing. People were dying, you figured out it was from a particular fish, you figured out where those fish were coming from, and you banned fishing in that pond. Ever since the ban, unexplained deaths have gone *way* down in Seenia. In this particular case, a ban was the right thing to do. You tried educating people first and that failed. Since the Carrot Fish looks so similar to the Parsnip Fish, both having three eyes and being the same shape, people were mistaking one for the other. With plenty of other safe ponds and rivers to fish in the area, you banned fishing in Zeleny Pond – a reasonable thing to do. And this wonderful town has been better off because of it.

"But the same can't be said about banning fire magic. I suppose an argument could be made for banning certain spells. But an entire type of magic? When fire magic was banned, it set an awful precedent. What's next: Wind magic? Water magic? Healing magic? It's a slippery slope, you see. Fire magic might be the first to get banned but, I'm telling you, it won't be the last. Before you know it *all* magic will be banned. What then? I've heard they're already taking about banning ice magic – maybe even *all* water magic – up in Ostaville. And when they do, you better believe Seenia's next. If we don't do something to stop the insanity plaguing our beautiful continent soon, before we know it, magic will be banned in all of Ravnia from the Northern Plains all the way down to Yoog. And it's not just magic. Some people are advocating the banning of certain weapons. Some fools are even calling for the banning of *all* weapons."

As Sandor spoke, Rhys and Malaric noticed a group of hooded figures gathering at the edge of the crowd. Though their faces and bodies were mostly hidden by the robes they wore, Rhys could tell they were of several races by their varying heights.

"Not these idiots again," a woman standing next to Rhys said under her breath.

"Who are they?" Rhys asked.

"Them?" the woman replied, subtly nodding toward the robed group. "They're SJWs."

"I don't know what that means," Rhys said. "What are SJWs?"

"Social judgment wizards. They use magic to bully anyone who doesn't agree with their views. I can't stand them. But don't tell anyone I said that."

Rhys returned his attention to Sandor, who turned his attention to the SJWs when he noticed them gathering just outside the crowd. They all began casting a spell at the same time.

"I see you," Sandor yelled at the SJWs. "I see what you're doing. You can silence me but you can't silence the tru-"

Sandor's lips kept moving but no sound came out. Though Rhys couldn't use magic himself, he'd adventured with enough wizards to know the SJWs cast some sort of silence spell on Sandor. The crowd, however, *could* still talk and the large group began getting loud and rowdy.

*I wonder if Sandor's right. I wonder if the fire-magic ban is what's causing it to snow up north. It makes sense, I guess. Too bad those social judgment wizards had to come along. I want to hear everything Sandor has to say. But it doesn't look like that's going to happen. Things are getting kind of crazy. Maybe we should get out of here.*

"I think we should probably go," Malaric suggested.

"I was just thinking the same thing," Rhys said. "Besides, it's almost time to meet Ena and Wynn. Come on."

They weaved their way through the crowd, which was getting wilder by the minute. Several crowd members yelled at the SJWs who'd begun casting another spell, but Rhys and Malaric didn't stick around long enough to find out what it was. They left the town center and headed toward the spot Ena and Wynn had agreed to meet them at. Along the way, Rhys and Malaric passed a number of people speed-walking toward the town center. Several of them were holding signs mostly written in Common. A dwarven man carried a sign that read *Ban All Blades!* A half-elven woman had a sign that simply read *Daggers=Death*. The last person Rhys and Malaric passed with a sign was a male gnome. His read *End Human Privilege* in four languages: Common, Elvish, Dwarven, and Gnomish – though Rhys could only read it in Common.

*Human privilege? That doesn't make any sense. I know several gnomes who are better off than any human I've ever met – except the king and queen, of course. And not just gnomes – elves, dwarves, and halflings, too.*

They got to the rendezvous point and waited for Ena and Wynn who showed up shortly thereafter.

"Did you two learn anything useful about snow, the cold, or anything the king and queen sent us to look into?" Rhys asked them. "Me and Mal just came from the center of town. There's a prophet named Sandor Perjonet who said that-"

"Tell it to us over a mug of ale and a big, meaty leg of... whatever," Wynn interrupted. "I'm starving. Let's tavern it up."

"Okay," Rhys agreed. "We can fill each other in at The Scene."

"The Scene isn't the only tavern in Seenia," Ena said. "Since we've already been there, you want to go somewhere else?"

"Whatever," Wynn replied. "As long as they have food and ale, it doesn't matter to me."

Ena looked at Rhys and Malaric. One nodded, the other shrugged.

"Then Obscene it is," she said and pointed. "This way."

The four adventurers walked halfway across town to Obscene. It was a smaller tavern than The Scene and the building was in much need of repair. Inside were a handful of patrons scattered about talking, eating, and drinking – mostly drinking. Unlike their experience at The Scene, the majority of tables were open. They sat down at one in the middle of the tavern and began talking. A server came over soon after.

"Welcome to Obscene – Seenia's oldest tavern," the human woman said.

"Wait a minute," Rhys replied. "I thought The Scene was the oldest tavern in Seenia."

"That's what they want you to believe," the woman said. "Obscene's been around much longer. But they don't acknowledge us because we refuse to cater to this town's nonsense – both literally and figuratively. The Scene's owner is sympathetic to the SJW's cause so they love it there. And he's got ties to lots of powerful people like the head of the water-magic school and Duke Tolkatel – the duke of Seenia. I even hear he's an anti-axer."

"What's an anti-axer?" Rhys asked.

"They're just one more ill-informed group of mindless followers. Like the morons who fought to abolish fire magic or the idiots who think daggers should be banned, anti-axers think-"

"Let me guess," Wynn interrupted. "They think axes should get banned."

"This one must be a scholar," the woman joked. Malaric chuckled. "Obscene is one of the last places in Seenia where reason and logic are allowed to flourish. And that's why they want to shut us down, just like they did to Sight Unseenia. The bastard who owns The Scene bought Sight Unseenia – what used to be a third tavern in Seenia, even older than this one – only to first *shut* it down, then *tear* it down. He's made several offers to buy Obscene but Larnyk, the owner, refuses to sell."

"Cool story," Wynn said. "Can I get a big, tall mug of ale? And something to eat, too."

A barely audible growl escaped from the woman's lips as she eyed Wynn up and down. After Rhys apologized for his friend, the server took everyone's order and left the table. While waiting, they traded stories about the day. Rhys was disappointed to hear Ena and Wynn hadn't learned anything new about snow. Eventually the server returned. They continued to chat while eating.

"I like this tavern better than the other one," Wynn said while chewing, a piece of mutton dangling from the corner of his mouth. It fell into his ale as he raised the mug to take a swig. "Their ale tasted like warm goblin piss compared to this stuff."

"I think I liked The Scene better," Malaric replied.

"You *would* like that place better," Wynn said, using his hand to wipe froth and mutton bits from his long, black beard.

"What's *that* supposed to mean?" Malaric asked.

"It doesn't mean anything," Rhys interjected. "He was just-"

*Bang!*

As Rhys tried to put an end to Wynn and Malaric's bickering for the millionth time, the tavern door burst open. Everyone in the tavern – including the adventures – stopped what they were doing and turned to the door. In rushed four townspeople carrying Sandor Perjonet. Rhys recognized a couple of them from the town center that afternoon. Blood covered Sandor's face and his once-flawless outfit. He had a big gash in his forehead and appeared to be unconscious.

"What's going on?" a tall, muscular human asked, running out from the kitchen. "What happened?"

"Sandor was giving a speech in the town center and things got out of control," one of the people carrying the injured scholar explained. "A bunch of SJWs showed up to silence The Prophet. But a group of pro-knifers came to his defense. Then more groups showed up. Before long it was chaos, Larnyk. Total chaos, I tells ya."

"But what happened to Sandor?" Larnyk asked. "How'd he get injured?"

"It was one of those crazy anti-sword activists. They whipped a big rock at Sandor and it hit him right in the head."

"Lay Sandor down here," Larnyk said, pointing to an empty table. While they did, Obscene's owner addressed the handful of patrons. "Is anyone in here a healer? Or does anyone at least have a healing potion?"

"I'm a healer," Malaric said and stood up.

"Can you heal this man?" Larnyk asked.

"I believe so," Malaric replied.

As Malaric went to work healing Sandor's head wound, everyone in the tavern heard sounds coming from outside. A group of people who'd been at the center of town gathered outside Obscene. After opening the front door a crack to take a peek, Larnyk closed and locked it.

"We know you're in there, Sandor!" someone yelled from outside. "You can't stay in there forever!"

Malaric finished casting a healing spell on Sandor. The scholar's eyes opened and everyone around him breathed a sigh of relief. But that relief was short lived. Outside the tavern, the group continued to grow. They began chanting and banging on the side of the tavern.

"Ban San!"

*Bang! Bang!*

"Ban San!"

*Bang! Bang!*

"Ban San!"

*Bang! Bang!*

"When did Seenia become Banborough?" Larnyk asked. "We can't just ban everything we don't personally agree with. That's no way to live."

"Ban San!"

*Bang! Bang!*

"It's only a matter of time until they get through the door," Larnyk said. "And when they do, there's no telling what they'll do to Sandor."

"I think I have a pretty good idea of what they'll do to him," Wynn said in between a bite of mutton and a swig of ale.

6.

"Ban San!"
*Bang! Bang!*
"Larnyk is-" Malaric uttered, then turned to the muscular human. "Am I saying that right? Larnyk?"

He nodded.

"Larnyk is right," Malaric continued. "That mob's going to tear Sandor apart if they get in here."

Wynn finished his ale, got up from the table, walked over to the bar, and slammed the mug down on the counter. Then he took his warhammer out from behind his back.

"Fill 'er up," Wynn said to the woman behind the counter, then turned his attention to the door. "I say we just open it and bash them one by one as they come in."

Wynn kissed the head of his warhammer and then began slapping it against his open hand over and over. Larnyk walked over to Wynn and put a hand on his shoulder. The two men were of roughly equal height and muscularity, though Larnyk was much older.

"I appreciate your enthusiasm, lad," Larnyk said. "But we can't just start smashing people as they come into my tavern."

"Why not?" Wynn asked, genuinely curious.

"Well, for starters it's bad for business. It's hard enough getting people in here these days. But if Obscene becomes known as the tavern that smashes your face in as soon as you walk through the door, even less people will come here."

"He's right," Rhys said, but knew Larnyk's

reasoning wouldn't cut it. "This is no place for face smashing. Nor is it a place for neck chopping or skull splitting. Look around. This is a small tavern. There's not enough room for you to get even a half-swing of your hammer."

"*War*hammer," Wynn corrected. "But now that you mention it, you're right. I won't be able to cave in any skulls here. I could definitely dent a few, though."

"I know you could, buddy," Rhys said to Wynn who'd finally been convinced to put his warhammer away. Then Rhys turned to Larnyk. "Is there any other way out of here besides the main entrance?"

Larnyk didn't answer. His eyes darted around the tavern and he locked his fingers together, squeezing tightly. Rhys didn't pick up on Larnyk's anxiety, but Wynn did.

"Ban San!"

*Bang! Bang!*

"What are you not telling us?" Wynn asked.

"If there's ever been a time to use it," the woman behind the bar said, "it's now."

Larnyk took a deep breath and exhaled slowly. He nodded to the woman.

"Use what?" Rhys asked.

"There's a secret way out of Obscene," Larnyk replied. "Will you traveling adventurers help me use it to get Sandor out of here?"

"Nope," Wynn said. He'd returned to his food at the table with the freshly poured mug of ale the woman behind the bar had given him. "I offered my help. You didn't want it. The people who brought him in can help."

"Come on, Wynn," Ena replied. "They're townies, not adventurers. Sandor needs our help – all of us."

He didn't respond, not that he could've. Wynn had a mouthful of mutton, some of which managed to escape out of the corners of his mouth as he chewed.

"Ban San!"

*Bang! Bang!*

The crowd outside Obscene grew larger and larger. Every *Ban San* was a little louder than the one before it. And the tavern walls shook just a little harder each time. It was clear to everyone inside that the door would be breached at any moment.

"Wynn!" Rhys yelled at his friend. "Now's not the time for this. We have to go."

"But I'm just finishing up my-"

"Now!" Rhys screamed.

"Fine, bro. Damn. You don't have to yell."

Wynn finally got up, taking a full leg of mutton and the now-three-quarters-full mug with him.

"Help carry Sandor and follow me," Larnyk said.

Rhys and Malaric helped Sandor off the table. Though conscious, The Prophet was still quite dazed from the blow to the head. They all followed Larnyk into the back room behind the counter. Wynn was the last to join them. He stopped at the bar to top off his mug.

"I don't see any exits," Rhys said.

"That's the point," Larnyk replied.

The tavern owner furiously began moving things around and the barmaid helped him. They took large pots, trays of mugs, and other random kitchen items off the floor and moved them to the counter. When they were done, a square section of floor in the back had been cleared.

"I still don't see any-" Rhys started to say.

Larnyk pulled open a drawer, reached way into the back of it, and pushed something. They all heard a click and the uncovered part of the floor popped open.

"Oh, never mind," Rhys corrected. "Yes I do."

Larnyk grabbed a lantern off a shelf in the kitchen, lit it, and walked over to the raised floor. Above it hanging on the wall was a sheathed two-handed broadsword. Before Larnyk had decided to settle down in Seenia and buy a tavern, he was a well-traveled fighter. He and that sword had a lot of history together. Larnyk took it off the wall and strapped it across the chest so the sword was on his back. He then pulled the floor all the way open, revealing a ladder leading underground. Larnyk started climbing down it.

"Follow me," he said to the adventurers, then looked at the barmaid. "As soon as we're all down the-"

"I know, I know," she said. "We've been over this a thousand times. Close the hatch and recover the floor."

Larnyk nodded and smiled at the barmaid. The adventurers followed him down the ladder. Malaric carried Rhys' equipment while Rhys threw Sandor over his shoulder and carried him. One by one, they all followed. Wynn was the last. He knew he couldn't go down the ladder carrying both his ale *and* mutton, so he had to make a choice. For Wynn, it was an easy one. He took a few last bites of mutton, then tossed the rest on the kitchen floor before heading underground. The barmaid scoffed. Following Larnyk's instructions, she closed the lid – whacking Wynn on the head – and quickly began covering the floor. As soon as she finished, the angry mob finally got the tavern door open and they all rushed into Obscene.

Underneath the tavern, the adventurers made it to the bottom of the ladder and were following Larnyk down a long tunnel. They'd all explored a few caves and even a couple of small dungeons before, but had never seen anything like it. Even Wynn was impressed.

"Did you build this, Larnyk?" he asked. "It must've taken forever."

"Yes and no," Larnyk answered as he led the group. "The tunnel was here when I bought Obscene. But it was much smaller, too small for anyone other than maybe a halfling or a child to fit through. I had a feeling it might come in handy someday, so I widened it and added the secret door."

"Impressive as it is," Rhys said, "I'd be more interested to know *why* you thought it would come in handy. And more importantly, where it leads to."

"I built it for situations exactly like the one we find ourselves in right now. And you'll learn where it leads soon enough. We're almost there."

Larnyk came to the end of the long underground tunnel. Like the ladder they'd all climbed down, there was another one going up.

"I sure hope she's home," Larnyk uttered under his breath but, in the small tunnel, everyone heard him.

"Hope *who's* home?" Malaric asked.

Larnyk climbed up the ladder and began knocking on the wooden door at the top. As soon as he did, they heard a click and the door opened.

"I had a feeling I'd be seeing you," an elderly woman said. "You had me starting to worry, what with all the commotion coming from your tavern."

Larnyk climbed up through the door and helped everyone who came after him. They were in another kitchen. But this one wasn't the kitchen of a tavern or other business. It looked like the kitchen of a little old lady – because that's exactly what it was.

"Oh my," the woman said when she noticed Sandor. Though the cut on his forehead had been healed by Malaric, his face and clothing were still covered in blood. Gradually, Sandor was starting to feel better. But he still needed Rhys to help him stand upright. "What happened to this one?"

"This is Sandor Perjonet, the Prophet of Karlov," Larnyk explained. "He was speaking in the town center when an angry mob attacked him and followed him to Obscene."

"Ooohhh," she replied. "I've heard of you. Nice to meet you Sandor Perjonet, Prophet of Karlov."

"Likewise. Though you've got me at a disadvantage," Sandor said. "And please: it's just Sandor. I'm not a prophet. I wish everyone would stop calling me that."

"My apologies. I'm Gwenith, though most just call me Gwen. And who are the other four?"

Malaric, Rhys, and Ena introduced themselves to Gwen. Wynn introduced her to his now-empty mug.

"I don't suppose you've got any ale, do you?" he asked. "Or wine. I'll drink wine, too. Mead if it's all you've got."

"Please excuse my rude friend," Rhys said. "His name is Wynn."

"Sorry, Wynn," Gwen replied. "I don't keep any alcoholic drinks on hand. They don't agree with my stomach." Wynn half sighed, half eye-rolled. She slowly waked over to a shelf and pointed to a jar filled with a green plant. "I do, however, have something else you might like. It makes my joints feel better and helps me relax. Really, it makes everything better – especially food."

Wynn's face lit up like a torch. But before he could reply, Larnyk started talking.

"We need to get Sandor out of Seenia as soon as possible. He's not safe here."

"He's safe in my house for now, but I get your point," Gwen replied.

"We're leaving Seenia in the morning to head north," Rhys said. "Sandor is welcome to travel with us if he's going that way."

"It would be much safer if you leave under the cover of darkness," Larnyk said. "Why don't you wait until the sun goes down tonight and then start heading north."

At first, there was some disagreement between the four adventurers. But eventually they all agreed – some more reluctantly than others – to leave Seenia after sundown.

"Do you want to come with us to make sure Sandor gets away safely?" Malaric asked Larnyk.

"I would," Larnyk replied. "But I need to take care of my tavern. Speaking of, I need to get back to make sure the mob doesn't destroy the place."

"Hypothetically speaking," Ena said, looking out one of Gwen's windows, "it if was already destroyed, would you come with us?"

Larnyk could tell by Ena's tone that there was nothing hypothetical about her question. He walked over to the window and Larnyk's face began glowing bright red. Part of it was from the anger boiling up inside him. But part was also from the glow of his beloved tavern burning to the ground just a few buildings down.

The majority of Obscene was made of old, dry wood and it went up quickly. Larnyk knew there was absolutely nothing he could do to stop the fire. The entire building was engulfed in flames. He only hoped the barmaid, handful of loyal patrons, and the ones who carried Sandor in were able to get out before it was too late.

The muscular man took a few steps over to a table in Gwen's kitchen. Larnyk collapsed in a chair and buried his face in his massive hands. No one said anything for a while. Even Wynn felt sympathy for the man who'd just lost his beloved tavern and kept quiet. Everyone just stood in the kitchen, occasionally glancing from one person to another.

"Why don't you all go make yourselves comfortable in the living room," Gwen eventually said to the adventurers and Sandor. "Give Larnyk a little time alone."

They all nodded and began walking out of the kitchen. But before they all left the room, Larnyk picked his head up and uttered a single sentence before faceplanting back into his palms.

"Tonight, I'll go with you."

7.

As soon as the sun set, Larnyk, Sandor, and the four adventures prepared to leave Seenia and head north into the mountains. Gwen gave Larnyk and Sandor long, hooded robes to wear to hide their identities on the way out of town. Sandor's robe fit his thin frame just fine. Larnyk's, however, was extremely tight and looked a bit silly on his tall, muscular body.

"Thank you for everything, Gwen," Larnyk said.

"Yes, thank you," Sandor added. "You've been most hospitable."

"You're very welcome – all of you," Gwen replied. "Safe travels."

The six of them left Gwen's house and hurried to the main road. It was dark and there weren't many people out and about. Only one of two moons were visible, sitting just above the horizon. It was about half full and provided just enough light to see. They got to the main road and headed north toward the Seenia Mountains. The group got to the edge of town and were beginning to think they'd made it safely out of Seenia. But then they heard someone behind them.

"Larnyk?" a man asked in a deep voice. "Is that you?"

Rhys glanced at Larnyk. It wasn't hard to imagine how someone might have recognized him. Larnyk was one of the largest humans in Seenia and the robe he wore left very little to the imagination. His thick arms and massive torso were practically busting out of of the thing. And the massive broadsword strapped to Larnyk's back made his identity even more obvious. When he heard someone call his name, Larnyk didn't stop – he walked even faster. The others did, too, though Sandor struggled to keep up with them.

"Halt!" the deep-voiced man yelled. "Stop at once and remove your hoods!"

They didn't stop *or* remove their hoods. The group walked even faster up the road, practically jogging.

"I am a guard of Seenia and you will obey my command. All of you halt at once!"

Though they all heard the command, none of them obeyed it. What the guard did next, half of Seenia heard. He pulled out a brass horn and blew into it as hard as he could.

*Bwa-bwa-bwaaaaaaaaa!*

"All guards to the northern entrance!" he shouted. "I've spotted Sandor and his accomplices! All guards, main road, northern entrance!"

Everyone ran as fast as they could. Sandor struggled to keep up with the rest of the group. Even Rhys and Wynn, who were both wearing chainmail armor and carrying heavy packs, moved faster than him. Sandor knew he was slowing the group down and that the guards would likely catch up to him eventually. They didn't call him The Prophet for nothing. Out of breath, he stopped in the middle of the road.

"You all go on without me," Sandor said, breathing heavily between every few words. "I can't keep running. Besides, it's me they want. They won't chase after you once they've got me."

"Fine by me," Wynn said. "See ya, old man."

Everyone stopped where they were. Footsteps – and lots of them – were coming up the road, getting closer by the second. It was too dark to see how many guards were chasing them, but they knew they'd find out soon enough.

"I refuse to let those guards lay a finger on you," Larnyk said, turning around and walking over to Sandor. The adventurer-turned-tavern-owner reached behind his back and pulled out his beloved broadsword, a weapon he'd used to slay countless monsters over the years. "If they capture you, they'll kill you. But I won't let you be silenced. Your message is too important."

Larnyk and Sandor could see two guards in the distance coming up the road. Everyone gathered together. As the two guards closed in on the group, they saw two more behind them.

"Take Sandor and get him out of here," Larnyk said. "I'll hold off the guards as long as I can."

For a moment, everyone remained silent and still. But they didn't have a moment to spare.

"I said go!" Larnyk yelled. "Get Sandor out of here. Now!"

Rhys gave Larnyk a hard pat on the back, then grabbed Sandor's hand, turned, and rushed up the road. He yanked the old man so hard that his hood came off. Ena and Malaric were right behind them. But Wynn stayed with Larnyk and pulled out his warhammer. Rhys quickly noticed that his friend stayed behind.

"Wynn," Rhys yelled as he continued up the road with Sandor, Ena, and Malaric. "What the hell are you doing?"

"Yeah, what the hell *are* you doing?" Larnyk asked.

"Keep going," Wynn yelled to Rhys. "I'll catch up to you shortly."

*But first, me and my warhammer are going to have a little fun. I've barely gotten to use this beautiful skull smasher.*

The first two guards got to Larnyk and Wynn. Both were carrying shortswords and wearing leather armor. Without hesitation, they drew their weapons and attacked.

*Cling! Clang!*

One of the guards swung at Larnyk, who blocked the attack with his broadsword. He countered, swinging the two-handed weapon as hard as he could. The guard raised his shortsword to block, but Larnyk's thick blade sliced right through it. Sparks shot in several directions and the tip of the shortsword flew off into the darkness, leaving the guard with a really-short sword.

The other guard lunged at Wynn, trying to stab him in the face. Wynn easily dodged the attack, jumping out of the way. He swung his warhammer at the guard but was still slightly off balance and missed.

Two guards turned into four as the other pair caught up to them. One had a shortsword and the other a dagger. They surrounded Wynn and Larnyk, slashing and stabbing away.

*Cling! Ching!*

Sparks flew as swords crashed into each other. The guard with the dagger lunged at Larnyk, who was busy defending against an attack from the one with the broken shortsword. Larnyk blocked the shortsword, but the guard with the dagger got him in his side. Unlike Wynn who was decked out in head-to-toe chainmail, Larnyk only had on a tunic, breeches, and the ill-fitting robe. The robe had already ripped in several places around his joints from swinging the broadsword. The guard with the dagger added another hole, but not just to the robe.

"Ugh," Larnyk moaned as blood poured from his side.

The dagger-wielding guard pulled back and a grin grew across his face. Then a warhammer smashed it in.

*Crunch!*

Blood shot out in every direction as Wynn's warhammer connected with the dagger-wielding-guard's face. The man dropped his weapon, which fell tip first and stuck in the ground, his lifeless corpse landing next to it.

"Ooooooh yeah!" Wynn yelled. "That's what I'm talking about!"

*Cling!*

While he was gloating, one of the guards swung his shortsword at Wynn's torso. It connected and knocked the wind out of him, but Wynn's armor blocked the blade from slicing his skin. At the same time, Larnyk swung his broadsword at the guard with the broken shortsword. He tried to block the attack, but failed. Larnyk's blade sliced clean through the guard's shoulder and his arm fell to the ground, fingers still wrapped around the hilt of his broken sword.

"Arrrggghhh!" the guard screamed, clutching at his shoulder.

He turned around and ran back toward Seenia, leaving a trail of blood along the way. Two down, two to go.

One of the guards tried to capitalize on Wynn taking a moment to refill his lungs and swung his shortsword. Wynn managed to raise his warhammer just in time to block the blade from connecting with his head. Even wearing the heavy chainmail helmet, Wynn knew it would've been devastating if it'd connected. That made him angry. He took a step back, wound up, and swung his warhammer as hard as he could.

*Caaarrrunch!*

Wynn's warhammer hit the guard's chest, dead center. Not only did it knock the wind *out* of him – the blow shattered several ribs sending pieces of bone *into* his lungs. The guard dropped his sword and fell to his knees, clutching his chest.

Larnyk and the other guard were going back and forth swinging away at each other. For a moment, they seemed to be evenly matched. Larnyk's weapon was stronger but slower, while the guard's was faster but weaker. He managed to slice Larnyk a couple of times, but not very deeply. Larnyk was going for a kill shot. He raised his broadsword high overhead and brought it down at the guard with all he had. The guard was mid-swing and didn't have time to defend against Larnyk's attack. What would turn out to be the guard's final swing was a good one. His shortsword sliced deep into Larnyk's leg. But then a fraction of a second later, Larnyk's blade connected with the guard's head, splitting his skull in half.

*Smash!*

Wynn finished off the guard who's chest he'd caved in a moment earlier by giving him a matching face. Three corpses and an arm surrounded Wynn and Larnyk.

"Man, am I glad I stayed back to get in on the action. I feel great!" Wynn said, then glanced at Larnyk. "But you don't look so good."

"I'll be fine," Larnyk replied, leaning to one side. "I've survived worse."

In addition to several small cuts all over his body, blood poured from Larnyk's side. And he had a deep gash in his thigh – also pouring blood – making it impossible for him to stand up straight.

*Clip, clop. Clip, clop. Clip, clop.*

"More guards," Larnyk said when they heard horses coming up the road.

"Yup," Wynn agreed. "More guards. Lots of them by the sound of it."

"Go."

"What?"

"I'll hold them off for as long as I can. I'm obviously not going anywhere," Larnyk said, nodding down at his leg. "But if we both stay, we'll both die. Go catch up to the others and get Sandor safely to Ostaville."

*Are you kidding me? I'm ready for more action! I could stand here caving in skulls all night long. But you're right. Those guards on horseback will be better equipped than these chumps. If I stick around, I'll likely be killed along with you. I bet I could cave in a lot of skulls before that happened, though.*

"Go!" Larnyk said again. "The Seenia Mountains aren't far from here. When you catch up with the others and get to the mountains, take the path that goes up them – not either of the roads that go around. The terrain is too rugged for the horses to climb up it. That'll be your best chance of getting to Ostaville safely."

*Clip, clop! Clip, clop!*

The horses were getting closer.

"It's been an honor killing with you," Wynn said, patting Larnyk on the shoulder.

"You as well. Safe travels."

"Give 'em hell," Wynn said, followed by one last pat.

He turned and ran as fast as he could up the road, leaving Larnyk behind. A couple minutes later, Wynn heard the unmistakable sound of metal on metal behind him. He stopped for a moment to listen. A horse cried out in pain, followed by a person doing the same. Wynn could tell it wasn't Larnyk's voice.

"That a boy, Larnyk," Wynn said out loud, smiled, then turned and continued running up the road.

The sound of fighting behind him continued for a while. Wynn was both happy and proud that Larnyk did, in fact, give them hell. But eventually the sound of metal on metal stopped and the sound of horses resumed. Soon after, Wynn finally caught up to the others just as they were getting to the edge of the Seenia Mountains.

"Where's Larnyk?" Rhys asked.

"Didn't make it," Wynn said, catching his breath. "Explain later. Over the mountain."

"What?" Ena asked. "Slow down."

"We have to go up and over the mountains, not around them. The horses won't be able to follow us."

The four adventures, along with Sandor, continued north and soon got to the path leading directly into the mountain range. With the sound of horses getting closer and closer, they left the main road and headed up the path.

8.

Everyone was glad when they no longer heard horses. They could tell the horses had broken up into two groups at the base of the mountain – one taking the road going west and the other taking the road going east. The sky was mostly clear, now with both moons visible, each about half-full. The moons provided enough light for the adventurers to continue up the path for a couple hours until they were sure it'd be safe to stop for the night. They found a small cave in which to set up camp. Rhys got a fire going and they all sat around it.

"It's a shame Larnyk died because of me," Sandor said.

"He died valiantly," Wynn replied. "There's no shame in that."

"I suppose," Sandor said.

Each adventurer agreed to take watch for a quarter of the night. Fortunately, it was an uneventful one and everyone slept soundly.

The next morning, they all continued up the mountain. The day went by without incident. The group didn't run into any monsters or other travelers along the path. Most adventurers and merchants chose to go around the Seenia Mountains rather than over them. It took a little longer but the terrain was flatter and easier to travel on.

When the group stopped for the night, they were near the top of the mountain. It was cold and windy. Rhys tried to get a fire going.

"We need to be on the lookout up here," Sandor warned.

"Oh yeah?" Malaric asked. "For what?"

"Monsters. There are powerful monsters that live up here at the top of the mountain."

"What kind of monsters?" Wynn asked, suddenly taking an interest in the conversation.

"The Abhorrent Mountain Man, for one," Sandor replied.

"I thought you were supposed to be a scholar," Wynn said. "Everyone knows the Abhorrent Mountain Man is just a myth. He's not real. It's just something parents tell their children so they don't go wandering off into the mountains."

"Perhaps," Sandor replied. "But there are other monsters up here that are definitely real. Several adventurers have spoke of encounters with two-headed beasts high up in these mountains. And of course there are mountain goblins. I'm surprised we haven't run into any, actually."

"We ran into some on our way from Krasnia to Seenia," Rhys said as he struggled to get a fire going.

"Give me that," Wynn said, taking the flint and steel from Rhys. "I'll show you how it's done."

Wynn didn't have any more luck getting a fire started than his friend. And neither did Malaric after him.

"I could always use magic to get a fire going," Ena suggested.

"I don't know if that's such a good idea," Rhys replied. "Fire magic is banned up here, remember?"

"Who's going to know?" Wynn asked. "Are *you* going to tell on her?"

"Of course not," Rhys replied. "But we already got ourselves into trouble by helping Sandor escape from Seenia. I just don't want to do anything that could make things worse."

"If we don't get a fire going somehow," Malaric said, "we're going to be in *real* trouble."

Rhys knew his friend was right. Sandor was shivering – they all were. But the old man shook so hard he looked like he might burrow into the mountain. Without a fire, Rhys knew there was a good chance they wouldn't all survive the night.

"Fine," he finally said. "Go ahead and use your magic, Ena."

From memory, she cast a basic fireball spell. As Ena neared the end of the incantation, she pointed at the firewood they'd assembled. Her finger shook so hard, one of the three fireballs that shot out of it nearly took Wynn's head off.

"Hey, watch it!" he yelled as a fireball whizzed past his head and into the side of the mountain.

"Sorry about that," Ena replied and shrugged.

The other two fireballs ignited the wood and everyone gathered around it to warm themselves. After a long day of traveling, they were all exhausted. Before long, everyone fell asleep except Ena who'd agreed to take first watch.

"Huh, that's strange," she said to herself.

Ena noticed that the tip of one of her fingers – the one she'd used to shoot the fireballs – was red. She examined it in the light from the fire and tried to rub off whatever had gotten on it. But whatever it was, it wouldn't come off. Ena wasn't very worried about it, though.

"Strange," she said again.

Ena's watch went by uneventfully, as did Wynn's and Malaric's. Rhys had agreed to take the forth-and-final watch. It had gotten even colder overnight. He had to sit so close to the fire to keep warm that, every so often when a gust of wind hit it just right, the flames singed the hair on his knuckles.

Rhys noticed the first sign of sunlight coming up over the horizon. It was beautiful – one of the most beautiful sights the young adventurer had ever witnessed. A quarter-smile grew across Rhys' half-frozen face as he looked out over the mountains. The wind died down for a moment, the air becoming silent and still. Then Rhys' face lit up, his quarter-smile morphing into an ear-to-ear grin.

"I don't believe it," he mumbled.

Rhys used his singed knuckles to rub his eyes, then opened them wide as he looked up at the sky. A snowflake gently fell from above, vanishing when it reached the heat from the fire. A few seconds later, another.

"Guys!" Rhys yelled, gradually getting up, his eyes glued to the sky. "Wake up!"

"Monsters?" Wynn asked, jumping right up. He was already in his battle stance, warhammer in hand, before Rhys had even fully gotten to his feet. "Where?"

Ena and Malaric also hopped up and grabbed their weapons, though not with nearly as much enthusiasm. Sandor awoke and sat up slowly.

"Not monsters," Rhys said. "Snow."

"What are you talking about?" Wynn asked.

"Snow," Rhys repeated, pointing up at the sky.

"Where?" Wynn asked. "I don't see anything."

"I don't see anything either," Ena added.

"I just saw – just a second ago," Rhys replied still looking up, his eyes darting all over the place. "White rain falling from the sky. I swear!"

"Sure ya did, buddy," Wynn said and dropped his warhammer, disappointed. He walked off to go relieve himself. "Sure ya did."

"I believe you," Malaric replied to Rhys.

"What did it look like?" Ena asked.

"It was breathtaking," Rhys answered, still trying to wrap his head around what he'd just seen. "Just like the stories we heard back in Krasnia. Little drops of white rain that fell slowly from the sky. Then they just kind of disappeared."

"Isn't that convenient," Wynn said as he walked back over to the others. "They disappeared before anyone else got to see them."

"I'm telling you," Rhys replied to his friend.

"I believe he's telling the truth," Sandor said. "His description is consistent with everything I've heard about snow."

"This coming from the so-called scholar who thinks the Abhorrent Mountain Man is real," Wynn snickered.

The sun came up over the horizon and the group prepared to continue heading north. Rhys had a hard time staying focused on gathering his gear, stopping every few seconds to look up at the sky.

*I can't believe it's real. I can't believe it's really real. I knew it. But now I know for sure. I just wish Wynn and the others could see it with their own eyes, too.*

Rhys' wish didn't come true. Aside from the few snowflakes he'd seen before the others were awake, no more fell from the sky that morning.

"What happened to your finger?" Rhys asked Ena as they walked along the path.

"What, this?" she replied, holding up her red pointer finger. "I don't know. I'm sure it's nothing to worry about."

"You're probably right."

The group traveled north all day long. They were now almost halfway down the mountain. The sun neared the horizon and they looked for a good place to camp for the night.

"Man, this really bums me out," Wynn said.

"What?" Rhys asked.

"We haven't run into any monsters up here. Not a one."

"And that's a bad thing?" Malaric asked.

"Not if you're a scared little chump like you," Wynn replied.

"I'm nearly as tall as you are," Malaric said.

"Fine. A scared *big* chump," Wynn said. "Hopefully we'll encounter some monsters tomorrow before we get to the bottom of the mountain."

"Unlikely," Sandor replied. "The only monsters known to exist in the Seenia Mountains are all at higher elevations where the air is most comfortable for them. We should be in the clear. If we were going to encounter any monsters, it would've happened already."

They found a small cave just as the sun was setting. Everyone agreed it would be a good place to spend the night. The air was much warmer and calmer than it had been the night before, but it was still cooler than they were used to. While a couple of them gathered wood and got a fire going, Rhys explored the shallow cave.

"Uh, guys?" Rhys said as he came out of it. "Some*one* or some*thing's* been in this cave recently."

"Why do you say that?" Ena asked.

"There's a half-eaten carcass in there, fairly fresh. Looks like it was a mountain goat. Whatever caught it tore it to pieces."

"A mountain lion, maybe," Malaric suggested.

"Maybe," Rhys agreed. "Whatever it was, it's not in there now. But it might return at some point, so-"

Rhys stopped talking when he heard something rustling in the trees not far from the cave. The others heard it, too. Whatever it was, it was big. Wynn readied his warhammer and Malaric pulled out a dagger.

"What is it?" Ena asked.

"I'm not sure," Rhys replied, cautiously walking toward the sound.

Wynn also slowly moved closer to where the sound was coming from. Though they'd gotten a fire going, the trees were thick and they couldn't see very far into them. The rustling got louder. Rhys reached behind his back and wrapped his fingers around the hilt of his longsword. But before he could draw his weapon, a massive beast leapt out from behind a tree and pounced on top of him.

*Slam!*

Rhys went flying, landing on his back. A two-headed monster jumped on him and slashed his face with its razor-sharp claws. Rhys held his hands up in front of his face to protect it and couldn't get a good look at the creature. But the others were able to see it just fine.

"What the hell is that thing?" Wynn asked, almost smiling as if happy to see it.

"Some sort of chimera," Sandor replied, taking cover on the other side of the fire.

"A what?" Wynn asked. "Ah, who cares. Die!"

Wynn swung his warhammer at one of the monster's heads – the one closest to him and farthest from Rhys. It had long, sharp teeth, pointed ears, large eyes, and was covered in yellowish-brown hair. The fire danced in the creature's pupils, which were thin, black slits. Its other head also had thin, black slits for eyes, but the similarities ended there. Green scales covered the head and neck, its eyes small and wide. The two heads shared one body, which wasn't covered in scales *or* hair – just thick, pink skin. Its hind legs were short with talons at the end. The monster's front legs were twice as long but half as thick. Each front paw had four razor-sharp claws sticking out of it – the ones on the left with Rhys' blood on them.

*Smash!*

Wynn's warhammer connected with the head he'd swung at. Much to his disappointment, it didn't kill the thing. But the monster's furry head did seem stunned.

"Get this thing off me!" Rhys yelled.

The beast took another couple swipes at Rhys' face with its massive claws. His face didn't take any more damage, but his hands got badly sliced up while trying to defend against the attack.

Ena began casting a spell, standing closer to Sandor on the other side of the fire than to Rhys and the chimera. But Malaric rushed at the creature. He'd pulled out his second dagger and lunged at it from behind. Before Malaric had begun studying the healing arts, he'd already amassed a number of useful rogue skills – the double-backstab being one of his favorites.

*Raaaaaaaaar!*

The chimera cried out in pain – from both heads – when Malaric leapt at it from behind and planted his daggers deep in the monster's back. He tried to pull them out, but the chimera began jumping around wildly and it sent him flying backward. Rhys finally saw his opening and rolled out from underneath the creature – but not before catching a talon to the forehead. It added yet another scratch to his face which was already covered in blood.

With both of Malaric's daggers sticking out of its back, the chimera turned to face the person who'd put them there. Malaric took out the only other weapon he had on him: a small knife. Malaric raised the knife to throw at the monster. But before he had a chance, the head covered in scales swung around to face him. It opened its mouth revealing not-one-but-two rows of jagged teeth. Malaric stepped back, hoping to avoid getting chomped. While the rogue-healer was happy the chimera didn't try to bite him, he wasn't thrilled by what it *did* do.

*Whoosh!*

After taking a quick-but-deep breath, the scaled head unleashed a big ball of fire at Malaric. The dexterous former-rogue managed to avoid a direct hit – but not an indirect one. Parts of Malaric's clothing caught on fire. He stopped, dropped, and rolled around on the ground trying to extinguish the flames.

Wynn went in for another swing. Landing in almost the exact same place as his last blow, the head of his warhammer struck the chimera in its fur-covered head. Wynn's swing was a little harder this time and it knocked the creature unconscious – part of it, at least. The furry head fell to the ground, but the rest of the beast still remained upright. The injured chimera thrashed around, dragging its unconscious head along. Blood poured from both dagger wounds. Its green-scaled head looked right at Wynn and opened its mouth.

Just as the chimera was about to shoot flames at Wynn, Ena finished her spell. She took aim at the creature with the same red finger she'd used to get a fire going at the top of the mountain. Then, the large beast turned to stone.

"Do what you do best, Wynn," Ena said.

"Drink?" he replied.

"Smash! And hurry before it goes back to normal."

"You don't have to tell me twice," Wynn replied and raised his warhammer high overhead.

"I feel like I just did," Ena mumbled, though Wynn didn't hear her.

*Crash!*

Wynn swung his warhammer at the chimera's body and the entire thing shattered into a million pieces. It wasn't the first time Wynn had smashed a magically-sculptured enemy. But to him, it was just as sweet as if it were.

"Finally, a little action on this cold-ass mountain!" Wynn said, kissing the head of his warhammer.

Malaric healed the cuts on Rhys' face and hands first, then his own burns. Confident there were no other monsters in the area, the group settled into the cave near the fire.

"I thought you said there were no monsters down here old man," Wynn said to Sandor. "You said the only monsters in these mountains were all at the top."

"To the best of my knowledge," Sandor replied, "that was true. I've never heard of chimeras coming this far down the mountain. But obviously, they have. The question is *why*. And I think the answer is the same as why you encountered mountain goblins far from their usual home. While they like the cool, mountainous air, it's been getting *too* cold lately, even for them. So they've had no choice but to relocate."

"Maybe," Wynn said. "Or maybe you were just wrong all along. Maybe chimeras do live down here and you just didn't know about it."

"Perhaps," Sandor replied.

"We should all get some rest," Rhys suggested. "We've had a long day and tomorrow isn't going to be any shorter."

Each adventurer took a turn keeping watch while the others slept. The night went by smoothly and without further incident.

9.

The next morning they continued heading north, down the mountain. It took them almost the entire day but eventually got to where the path reconnected with the main road.

"Maybe we should camp for one more night and then head into town in the morning," Rhys suggested.

"Or maybe," Wynn replied, "since we're so close we can actually see Ostaville in the distance, we should spend the night eating hot food, drinking cold ale, and sleeping in an actual building where we're not freezing our balls off."

Ena scoffed.

"Freezing our balls *and titties* off," Wynn corrected. "Is that better?"

Ena scoffed again, this time shaking her head as well. Secretly, though, she found Wynn's comment – like so many others of his – to be at least a little humorous.

Rhys looked around to see who they agreed with more. Though each wished they didn't, all of them agreed with Wynn.

"We could all use a hot meal," Malaric said.

"It *has* been getting awfully cold at night," Ena added.

Rhys looked at Sandor. Then everyone else did, too.

"It's probably best if we head into town tonight while it's dark," Sandor said. "Some people in Ostaville like me even less than they do in Seenia."

"Then why the hell did we bring you here?" Wynn asked.

"Because not everybody hates me. I have friends in Ostaville I'd trust with my life. But it'd probably be best to get me into town and to the inn without anyone recognizing me. Tonight while it's dark is our best bet."

"Fine," Rhys agreed. "We'll head into Ostaville tonight. Let's get going."

Sandor put his hood on and they walked up the main road to Ostaville. By the time they'd arrived in town, the sun was well-over the horizon. Along the way to the inn, the group passed several people on the road. Some said hello, others nodded. But none of them noticed Sandor.

Along the sides of the road at the southernmost part of town were two large wooden signs – one on each side. The one on the left read *Welcome To Ostaville!* written in Common, Dwarven, Elvish, Halfling, Gnomish, and a few other languages none of them recognized. The slightly smaller sign on the right side of the road – written only in the common language – read:

The use of ALL fire magic is strictly prohibited.

Bladed weapons are not allowed in any public buildings or in the duke's castle.

ALL weapons must be sheathed at ALL times when on ANY main road.

Failure to follow these rules will result in fines, torture, death and, in some cases, worse.

Ostaville was huge – several times larger than Seenia. Aside from Sandor, none of them had ever been there before. As they walked up the main road looking for an inn, their eyes bounced back and forth between one side of the road and the other. There was a lot to see. On the outskirts of town were small houses and farmland, not unlike the other towns they'd been to. But as the group got closer to the center of Ostaville, the buildings got bigger and looked to have been built a lot more recently. Various signs were posted in people's yards. The signs in yards on the outskirts of town said things like *Being Human Is Not A Crime, Swords Don't Kill People – People Kill People,* and *My Magic, My Choice.* But as they got closer to the center of town, the group saw signs that said things like *End Human Privilege, Maces=Murder,* and *Magic Is Tragic.*

"Maces equal murder?" Wynn said as they passed them. "Now that's my kind of sign."

"You're against the use of maces?" Sandor asked.

"Against maces? What are you talking about? Maces are awesome. Maybe not as awesome as my warhammer but-"

"That's an anti-mace sign," Ena said.

"That doesn't make any sense," Wynn replied. "Maces *do* equal murder. That's the whole point of having a mace."

The group eventually found an inn at the center of town located right next door to a large tavern. They all got rooms and prepared to go next door for food and drinks – all but Sandor.

"You sure you don't want to come with us?" Wynn asked. He reached behind his back and tapped the head of his warhammer. "I'll protect you if anything happens."

"Not with that you won't," Rhys said.

"And why not?" Wynn asked.

"You saw the sign along the road," Rhys replied. "No weapons allowed in public buildings."

"It said no *bladed* weapons," Wynn said. "It didn't say anything about blunt weapons."

"Thank you," Sandor said to Wynn. "But I think it'd be best if I stayed here. Besides, I have a speech I need to work on."

"Suit yourself, old man," Wynn replied. "Now let's go get some food. I'm starving."

Agreeing to bring Sandor back something to eat later, the four adventurers walked next door to the tavern. A big sign hung above the door that read *The Bern Tavurn*.

"Somebody could use a Common lesson," Wynn said and laughed, looking up at the sign before entering the tavern.

The place was packed. Once in the door, the four of them just stood there looking around. The Bern Tavurn was larger than any of the taverns they'd been to in Seenia or Krasnia. Rows and rows of packed tables filled the room. A long bar went all the way up the right side of the room, then made a ninety-degree turn and went along the entirety of the far side. Bar stools ran along the bar, most with someone sitting on them. The crowd was quite diverse. At least a few members of every friendly humanoid race seemed to be at The Bern Tavurn. There were even three-or-four people of races none of them had ever seen before. Two waitresses – one human and one elven – rushed around from table to table carrying trays of food and drinks.

After soaking in the scenery for a moment, they found an empty table on the far side of the tavern and sat down. A minute later, a dwarven man came out from behind the bar and over to their table.

"Welcome to The Bern Tavurn," he said with a smile.

"Thank you," Rhys replied. "Would you please get one of the waitresses? We're starving."

"My name is Cedric and I'll be your server," he said, his smile getting a little smaller.

"*You* are our server?" Wynn asked with slanted eyebrows.

The dwarf's smile almost completely disappeared.

"What Wynn means," Ena said to Cedric, "is that we've never had a server like you before."

"Oh, I see," the waiter replied, leaning to the side with crossed arms, smile gone. "You think that because I'm a man I can't be a good server?"

"Ridiculous," Wynn replied. "If anything, that probably makes you a better server."

Ena stomped on Wynn's foot under the table with the heel of her boot. He did his best to hide the stabbing pain it sent radiating up his leg. Malaric chuckled.

"I apologize for my friend," she said. "What he means is, where we're from, all of our servers are either human or elven. We've never had a dwarven server before."

"Ohhhhhh," the waiter replied, uncrossing his arms. "I see. And where are you from?"

"Krasnia," Rhys answered.

"Well, here in Ostaville, anyone can be anything," Cedric explained. "We don't discriminate based on race, class, gender, or anything else. Not in Ostaville and especially not within these four walls. At The Bern Tavurn, everyone is equal."

"About that name," Malaric said. "Is there a reason why it's called The Bern Tavurn?"

"There is, actually," Cedric replied. "Before fire magic was banned in Ostaville, this tavern burned down several times. If I'm remembering correctly, it's been rebuilt four times since I was little."

"And all four of those times magic was the cause of the fire?" Ena asked.

"You know," Cedric replied, "I'm not sure. I suppose it could've been."

"Thanks, but that's not what I'm asking," Malaric said. "I'm not asking why it's called The Bern Tavurn. I'm asking why it's spelled that way."

"Ohhhhhh," Cedric replied. "You noticed, huh? Ostaville, being the forward-thinking town that it is, used a diverse group of people to rebuild the tavern the last time it burned down. Dwarves, humans, elves, gnomes, half-orcs, and others helped to build this wonderful place. However, most of the workers were male and not one was a halfling. So they hired a female halfling to make the sign hanging above the door out front, even though Ostaville has an experienced human sign maker. Unfortunately, the halfling woman doesn't read and write so well. As you noticed, she mixed up the U and the E. But the tavern owner didn't want to hurt her feelings. So instead of asking her to fix it, he decided to change the name of his tavern – change the spelling, anyway."

"Oh wow," Malaric said. "That's fascinating. I love how inclusive and progressive this town is."

Rhys and Ena both looked at Wynn, expecting him to say something. His foot still throbbing, Wynn didn't say a word.

Cedric took their orders and left the table. They talked among themselves until he returned carrying a large tray in his muscular hands a little while later. The server went around the table giving each of them their food and drinks.

"Ohhh yeah! Nuttin' but mutton," Wynn said as the dwarf placed a big plate of meat in front of him. "And ale, of course. Lots of ale."

"Last but not lesser," Cedric said to Ena, the only one he hadn't yet served, "roasted rabbit and a glass of wine."

He put Ena's food down in front of her, then just stood there for a moment staring. Like Wynn, Rhys, and Malaric, she was very hungry and started eating right away. None of them – not even Ena – seemed to notice Cedric gawking at her.

"What's that?" the dwarf asked Ena.

"You should know," she replied with a mouthful of rabbit meat. "You're the one who just gave it to me. It's rabbit."

"No, not that," Cedric said, then pointed at Ena's red finger. "*That*."

"Oh, that," she replied, swallowed, and took a sip of wine. "It's no big deal, really. I think it's just a little blood from a cut."

"I'd be happy to clean it for you," Cedric offered. "Give me your hand."

"Thank you, but that's not necessary."

"I insist," Cedric said, stepping even closer to Ena.

"She said she doesn't want you to clean it," Wynn said. A few pieces of mutton had fallen into his beard and they moved up and down as he talked. "So you're not going to lay a finger on her... finger. Now leave us alone so we can eat in peace. Actually, bring me another mug of ale, would ya?"

Cedric crossed his arms and just stood there for a moment, eyeing each of them. Then the dwarf dropped his arms and walked over to a nearby table. Sitting there were four men: a human, an elf, a half-elf, and a dwarf – all of them large and wearing heavy armor bearing the town's insignia. The symbol consisted of three items in a circle: a sword, a lightening bolt, and a hawk's head – all of them looking and pointing to the left. Cedric whispered something in the half-elf's ear. The tan half-elf's eyes darted from Cedric to the table the four adventurers were at, then back to Cedric. After a brief pause, the half-elf leaned over to the human next to him and whispered something in his ear. The human motioned for the elf sitting across from him to lean over the table and whispered something to him. Then, the elf whispered something to the dwarf next to him.

The half-elf stood up first, followed by the other three men. They followed Cedric over to the table where the adventurers sat.

"Excuse me, kind strangers," the tall, lean half-elf said. "I'm Sir Adeleath, sheriff of Ostaville, knighted by Duke Youngvalor. And these are my men."

"We're not interested in whatever you're selling," Wynn replied with so much mutton in his mouth they could barely understand him. He didn't even look up from his plate. "Fuck off."

One of Adeleath's men, the human next to him, reached for his longsword. Adeleath grabbed the man's arm, looked him in the eyes, and slowly shook his head. Reluctantly, the human relaxed his arm.

"I thought you weren't allowed to have bladed weapons in public places like this," Rhys said.

"You thought correct. *You* aren't allowed to have bladed weapons in here. But *we* are," Adeleath replied to Rhys, then turned his attention to Ena. "If you would, m'lady, kindly place your hands on the table so I may inspect them."

Ena had been hiding her red-fingered hand under the table ever since Cedric noticed it. She'd been awkwardly eating with only one hand.

"See?" Ena said, holding up the rabbit-guts-covered hand.

"*Both* of your hands," Adeleath insisted. "Place *both* of them at the edge of the table so that I, Sir Adeleath, sheriff of Ostaville, may inspect them."

Reluctantly, Ena placed her hands on the table. Adeleath's men gasped when they saw the red finger. The sheriff leaned over and examined it closely.

"See?" Cedric said. "I told you!"

As word traveled from table to table, barstool to barstool, the entire tavern got quiet. Four more men wearing armor bearing Ostaville's insignia got up from a table on the other side of the room and joined the others.

"You're going to have to come with us," Adeleath said to Ena.

"Why?" Rhys asked.

"For the use of forbidden fire magic. By the power granted to me through the duke of Ostaville, granted to him through the king and queen of Ravnia, I'm hereby placing you under arrest."

With fire in his eyes, Wynn stood up. But one of the large, armored men behind him easily and immediately sat him back down, pushing Wynn by the tops of his shoulders.

"But we are on a quest for the crown, for His Royal Majesty and Her Royal Highness!" Rhys protested.

"You could be on a quest for Xamos himself for all I care. I've got a job to do," Adeleath replied to Rhys, then offered a hand to Ena. "M'lady, if you would please accompany me out of the tavern."

Ena slowly chugged – more like quickly sipped – the half-glass of wine she had left. Adeleath's hand remained extended, though his patience grew thinner by the second. As Ena finished her wine and put the glass down, she glanced around the table. Ena could see fear and helplessness in all three of their faces. She could also see anger in Wynn's, though Ena assumed it had less to do with her and more to do with the large man who'd just forced him down in his seat. You'd never know it by looking at her, but Ena was terrified. She gracefully stood up without the assistance of Adeleath's hand, her mind racing.

*Where are they going to bring me? What are they going to do to me? It can't be that bad, can it? It's not like I used fire magic to burn down a castle or a statue of Xamos. I only used it as a last resort because we couldn't get a fire going. We would've froze to death if I hadn't. And it's my first offense, which means they'll probably go easy on me. I wonder how many others have been convicted of using illegal fire magic?*

Adeleath and his three men led Ena to the door. Just before exiting The Bern Tavurn, Adeleath turned and flicked a gold piece to Cedric.

"Your food and drinks are on the house as always, Sir Adeleath," Cedric said.

"It's to pay for *their* food and drinks," Adeleath replied, pointing to the three remaining adventurers at the table. "For any inconvenience this might have caused for this woman's *lawful* associates."

"But a gold is more than their meals cost, even with drinks," Cedric said.

"The rest is for you, good sir, for letting me know we had a criminal in our midst."

"I'm not a criminal!" Ena protested.

"Make sure the others don't try to follow us to the castle," Adeleath said to the four guards who'd gotten up and joined them from another table. They all nodded.

Adeleath and his three men left The Bern Tavurn with Ena. As soon as the last one was out, chatter began spreading around the room. The other four guards stood in front of the door for a few minutes to make sure Rhys, Malaric, and Wynn didn't chase after Ena. They didn't. The three of them just sat there silently, well-aware that half the room was staring at them. The guards eventually returned to their table once they were sure no one was going after Ena.

"Can I get you anything else?" Cedric asked the three remaining adventurers with a big, stupid grin on his face.

10.

The next morning, Rhys, Malaric, Wynn, and Sandor stood outside the inn talking about what'd happened the night before. None of them were fully dressed except Sandor – he was wearing the same robe Gwen had given him, hood up. Wynn was almost fully *un*dressed. He wore nothing but a short pair of stained breeches that only went halfway to his knees.

"We have to do *some*thing," Rhys said. "We have to at least *try* to get Ena back."

"That'd be a fool's errand if I've ever heard of one," Sandor replied.

"So you think we should do nothing?" Wynn asked. "Well, *you* can do nothing. Me, I'm going to smash in that guard's face who pushed me down at the tavern last night. Then I'm going to do the same to all the others who took Ena."

"That would be fitting for you," Sandor replied. Wynn started to smile. "It's even more of a fool's errand."

"Did you just call me a fool, old man?" Wynn asked, walking over to Sandor, smile gone.

Rhys stepped in front of Sandor before Wynn got over to him. He didn't think Wynn would've actually done anything to the frail scholar. But with Wynn, you never knew.

Before Wynn got anywhere near Rhys *or* Sandor, all of them heard someone around the corner. Wynn stopped in his tracks and they all turned to face the direction the sound came from. Even though they all heard him coming, when an elven man walked around the corner, several of them jumped.

"Whoa," the elven man said, holding his hands up. "I didn't mean to startle you."

"You didn't startle *me*," Wynn replied, though he'd jumped just as high – maybe even a little higher – than the others.

"We're in the middle of discussing something important," Rhys said to the elf. "So if you don't mind..."

"Is that some*thing* actually a some*one* – your elven friend who got taken out of The Bern Tavurn last night by Sir Adeleath and his men?" the elf asked.

"How do you know about that?" Wynn asked. "*What* do you know about it?"

"A lot more than you, by the sound of it. I wasn't eavesdropping, but I could hear you talking as I walked over."

"Who are you?" Malaric asked. "And what do you know?"

"How rude of me," the elf replied. "I'm Iolas, a forester. Although in some parts of Ravnia, they refer to people like me as a rangers. I was at The Bern Tavurn last night when your friend got taken away by Adeleath and the others."

"Do you know where Ena is or what they're planning to do to her?" Rhys asked. "How can we get her back?"

"I hate to be the one to tell you this," Iolas replied. "But in all likelihood, you won't be getting her back. Not alive, anyway. They might let you keep her corpse after the execution. But even that I doubt."

"Execution?" Rhys asked, almost laughing. He didn't think there was anything funny about Ena being executed, but found it absurd she'd be killed for lighting a fire to avoid freezing to death. "There's no way she'll be executed. She barely did anything wrong. Do you know where they're keeping her?"

"While you and I might think your friend did nothing wrong," Iolas explained, "Duke Youngvalor will undoubtedly have a different opinion. She's the first person to be accused of using fire magic since it's been banned. The duke will want to make an example out of her. And she's almost definitely being held in the castle to the east of Ostaville. Well, *under* the castle in one of its many dungeons."

"Could we bust Ena out?" Wynn asked.

"No," Iolas replied, bluntly. "Even if you managed to get *into* the castle, there's no way any of you would get *out*. The place is crawling with MAKs and other knights, armed guards, unarmed guards – I've heard they even have an armed one-armed guard. Any attempt to rescue your friend from the castle will fail. However..."

"Yes?" Rhys asked.

"Go ahead," Malaric said.

"I may be able to help," Iolas continued. "I'm part of a small group of rebels here in Ostaville who are fighting against some of the absurd changes that have been made recently."

"You're a member of Rising Shadow?" Sandor asked, his hood still hiding the entirety of his face.

"That's right," Iolas replied, his eyes lighting up, head tilting slightly to the side. The elf was clearly surprised. "So you've heard of us?"

"No. No, I haven't heard of you," Sandor stated. "That would be like saying Xamos has heard of Ravnia. I *created* you. Well, *co*-created. I'm one of Rising Shadow's founding members."

Iolas stepped closer to Sandor. The elf bent down, trying to see into his hood.

"Sandor Perjonet?" Iolas asked. "The Prophet of Karlov? Is that you?"

Sandor pulled his hood back slightly so Iolas could see his face. Then, he promptly covered it back up.

"Shhh," Sandor said. "Don't say my name so loud. But yes, it's me: Sandor of Karlov, though I don't like the prophet part."

Now more than just Iolas' eyes lit up. The elf's entire face glowed and his body looked like it was vibrating.

"Do any of the other Rising Shadow members know you're in Ostaville?" Iolas asked, keeping his voice down.

"No. We just got in last night."

"Then we should go see Braylin at once," Iolas said.

"That's precisely what I was just about to suggest to my associates before you arrived. Iolas, meet Wynn, Malaric, and Rhys."

After Wynn, Malaric, and Rhys threw on their gear, Iolas and Sandor led them away from the town center where the inn was located and toward the northern outskirts of Ostaville. They noticed that there weren't nearly as many signs in people's yards to the north of town as there were to the south. Eventually, they arrived at a large farm way up on the edge of Ostaville, just south of where the Northern Plains began.

"*This* is where the rebellion leader lives?" Wynn asked and laughed. "What's he going to do: harvest his way to victory?"

"She," Iolas corrected. "Braylin is a woman. And she could out-harvest you any day."

A modest house sat in the middle of the the property with acres of farmland surrounding it on all sides. With Iolas leading the way, they walked up to the front door. He knocked on it in a strange pattern: four times fast, three times slow, fast twice, then finished it off with one loud, closed-fist thump. The door opened – but just a little. An attractive human woman poked her head out. When Wynn saw her, he stood up straight – even straighter than usual – with his shoulders back and chest out.

"Who are your friends, Iolas?" Braylin asked from behind the door.

"These three are adventurers from Krasnia sent to Ostaville on an official quest by the king and queen."

"And you brought them *here*?" Braylin asked with lowered eyebrows, her face turning reddish-purple. "Why in the name of Xamos would you do such a thing?"

"Because of who they're with," Iolas replied, pointing to Sandor.

The old man pulled back the hood enough for Braylin to see his face. Her own face immediately returned to its normal color and a smile grew across it when she saw who'd been hiding under the hood.

"Please," Braylin said, holding the door open. "Come in."

The second they were all inside and she closed the door, Braylin threw her arms around Sandor. Immediately following the lengthy hug, Braylin shook one of Sandor's hands with both of hers.

"It's good to see you, old friend," Braylin said. "I can't believe you're here."

While everyone else stood in a circle, Wynn wandered around the living room. It looked like a perfectly average farm house to him – certainly not the home of a rebellion leader. While Wynn wandered, the others explained to Braylin what had happened to Ena. Wynn found his way back over to them just as they wrapped up.

"I agree with Iolas' assessment," Braylin said. "As the first wizard caught red-fingered using fire magic, your friend will be used as an example."

"I still find it hard to believe they'd execute Ena for nothing more than trying to stay warm," Rhys replied.

"So naive," Wynn uttered out of the corner of his mouth. Everyone heard him.

"Ena's not going to be executed because she was trying to stay warm," Braylin said. "Not even because she used fire magic. Your friend will be executed because she defied an official order from the duke of Ostaville. And since Ena's the first to defy said order, the duke needs to set a precedent – one so severe that no one else will dare to break the no-fire-magic rule."

Rhys still didn't want to believe anything tragic would happen to Ena. But after Braylin, Sandor, Wynn, and even Malaric took turns explaining why it's likely true, Rhys eventually came around. And as soon as he did, he started freaking out.

"I can't believe this," Rhys shouted. "I told Ena she shouldn't use fire magic when we were in the Seenia Mountains. If only I'd been more-"

"Relax and take a deep breath," Braylin interrupted, putting her hand on Rhys' shoulder. "This is actually a good thing."

"How can you say that?" Rhys asked. "How is it good that Ena's going to be put to death?"

"It's good because the execution will undoubtedly be a public one."

"How is *that* good?" Rhys asked.

"If your friend was being executed privately – like most people who get caught breaking a serious law, upsetting someone in power, or whatever – there'd be no way to save her. The castle where she's being held is overflowing with armed knights, wizards, and other guards. Even if we got in, we'd never get out. But since the duke will definitely want to make an example out of the first person to violate his fire-magic ban, Ena will be executed in the town center. And when they bring her from the castle to the center of town, it'll give us a chance to rescue her."

"Surely she'll be escorted by heavily armed guards," Rhys said. "There's no way the three of us will be able to rescue Ena by ourselves."

"You're right," Braylin agreed.

Rhys sighed, exhaling slowly.

"But with the help of Rising Shadow," Braylin continued, "you've got a chance."

"So you'll help us?" Rhys asked, eyes widening just a little.

"That's what she *just* said. Try to keep up. Jeez," Wynn replied to Rhys, then turned to Braylin, looking around the house. "No offense, but how could *you* possibly help?"

"Rising Shadow is a small-but-dedicated group," she replied. "Some of our members are highly skilled. And there are a lot of people around town who believe in our cause – they just can't admit it publicly."

"Why not?" Rhys asked. "What are they afraid of?"

"The MAKs, mostly," Braylin answered. "But more recently, ANTIMA."

"The who? And what?" Rhys asked. The others – aside from Sandor who already knew about them – were curious, too.

"Magical-adherence knights or MAKs for short," Braylin explained. "They enforce the magic bans that are already in place. It sounds like you met a few MAKs at The Bern Tavurn last night. Everyone's afraid of them."

"And what was the other one?" Rhys asked.

"ANTIMA. It's short for anti-magic. They want to ban *all* magic."

"Bunch of hypocrites," Sandor said.

"How so?" Malaric asked.

"They use the very thing they say they're against – magic – to push their misguided opinions on others," Sandor explained. "Between ANTIMA and the MAKs, everyone in Ostaville is afraid to say or do anything that goes against them."

"*Almost* everyone," Braylin corrected. "The members of Rising Shadow aren't afraid. In fact, we've been preparing for something like this. Your friend's public execution will be the perfect opportunity for us to strike."

"But we don't know when it'll be," Rhys said.

"Yes we do," Braylin replied, lightly tapping the tips of her fingers together. "Public executions are only held four times a year in Ostaville – at high noon the day after a double-full moon."

"And when's the next double-full moon?" Rhys asked.

"In three days," Braylin answered. "So we've got four days until the execution."

11.

The next morning, Rhys, Malaric, and Wynn went to the tavern to get some breakfast. Braylin told them to keep staying at the inn and to go about their quest for the king and queen.

"I still think we should've stayed with Braylin," Wynn said with egg yolk dripping from his beard. "She let Sandor stay with her."

"You heard what she said," Rhys replied. "The king and queen have eyes and ears all over Ostaville. We have to go about our quest as we normally would. For the plan to work, we can't let it be known we're in contact with anyone from Rising Shadow. That's why Braylin told us – told *you* – we couldn't stay at her farm house."

"For the plan to work?" Malaric said. "What plan? There is no plan."

"There is. We just don't know it yet," Rhys replied. "We'll find out the night of the double-full moon. That's when Braylin said she'd contact us with the details. But we're not supposed to go to her farm or try contacting her before then."

They finished eating and headed out on the town to continue with their quest talking to people about snow. The townsfolk were quite divided. Some of them insisted that snow was real. Many even claimed to have seen it with their own two eyes. However, a lot of Ostaville residents found the idea of snow preposterous. These people were unaffectionately called *snow deniers* by those who believed in it.

"I want to stop at the magic shop," Malaric said as they walked along the main road. "It should be coming up soon."

"Good," Rhys replied. "That'll give us a chance to see what the owner thinks about snow, the fire-magic ban, and everything else."

Sure enough, they soon got to the magic shop. Right when they arrived, four heavily armored MAKs were leading a half-elf out the front door.

"I didn't sell any fire magic," the half-elf yelled. "I swear! Not since the ban at least."

"So you admit to selling fire magic before the ban," one of the MAKs said, then pushed the half-elf. "Let's go."

The half-elf saw Malaric, Wynn, and Rhys walking toward his shop as the MAKs led him away from it. He waved his free arm – the other being held tightly by one of the magical-adherence knights – and shouted to them.

"I'm closed right now. Come back later!"

"For you, Yorlumin," the MAK holding his arm said, "there'll be no later."

"What do you mean there'll be no later?" the half-elf asked. "What are you going to do to me? I have a wife and kids. What are they supposed to..."

The MAKs escorted the half-elf away until his voice could no longer be heard. Rhys, Wynn, and Malaric stood in front of the magic shop, watching them disappear down the road.

"What are you doing?" Rhys asked when Malaric walked over to the door.

"I need supplies," he answered. "That was the whole point of coming here."

"You can't just steal them," Rhys said.

"Why not?" Wynn replied. "It doesn't look like the half-elf is going to need them."

Rhys opened his mouth to protest, but nothing came out. It wasn't everyday that Wynn agreed with Malaric. Rhys decided to let it go.

Malaric glanced up and down the road to make sure no one saw him. While the magic shop was located along the main road, there weren't any buildings next to or across from it. After seeing Malaric do it, Rhys also looked up and down the road to double check. The coast was clear. Malaric opened the door and slipped into the magic shop. Then Wynn started to follow.

"What are *you* doing?" Rhys asked him. "You can't use magic."

"Maybe not. But I *can* smoke the magic herb they have at some of these shops," Wynn replied and walked in.

Rhys looked up and down the road once more, then followed his friends into the magic shop. The scent of potent plants and powerful potions blasted him in the face as soon as he walked through the door. Malaric went behind the counter and began looking through the merchandise.

"See any of that green, skunky herb I like back there?" Wynn asked.

"What, this?" Malaric replied and held up a small leather pouch.

Wynn walked over to the counter, took the pouch from Malaric, and opened it under his nose. He inhaled deeply and a big, stupid grin grew across his face. But it vanished just as quickly as it'd appeared. Wynn froze in place and so did the others when they heard movement coming from out back. All three of them stayed perfectly still, their eyes glued to the door behind the counter where the sound came from. It was only open a crack and none of them – not even Malaric who stood closest to the door – could make out what it was.

"Hello?" Rhys asked.

No response.

Wynn closed the pouch and stuffed it into his bag, then pulled out a knife. Cautiously, he approached the door to the back room.

"I'll check it out," he whispered.

"Right behind you," Rhys replied. He took out his own knife and followed.

Wynn slowly pulled the door open and stepped into the back. Rows of shelves going all the way up to the ceiling filled the large room, which was several times bigger than the area out front. Books, gemstones, plants, powders, potions, and other magic-related items filled the shelves, making it impossible to see from one aisle to the next. Again, they heard movement. It seemed to be coming from the far corner of the room.

"Hello?" Rhys asked again.

Nothing.

Rhys followed Wynn, slowly going from aisle to aisle. They finally got to the last row where the sound was coming from. It had to be: all the other aisles were clear. Wynn re-wrapped his fingers tightly around the handle of his knife and walked around the corner. Then, Wynn suddenly lunged forward, disappearing from Rhys' sight.

"Aaaaaahhhhhh!" someone screamed in a high-pitched voice.

Rhys rushed around the corner with his knife in hand, ready for action. He stopped abruptly, nearly tripping over Wynn. Rhys was surprised to see his friend kneeling down in the aisle in front of two children, a boy and a girl. When the girl saw Rhys appear with a knife in his hand just like Wynn had a moment earlier, she screamed a second time.

"Aaaaaahhhhhh!"

"Where's our dad?" the boy asked, jumping in front of his sister to protect her from the two knife-wielding maniacs. "Did they take him?"

Wynn glanced up at Rhys. Though his friend looked relaxed as can be, Rhys' heart was nearly beating out of his chest. He still had his knife held out in front of him. Wynn grabbed Rhys' arm and guided it to his side.

"Did *who* take him?" Rhys asked, trying – and failing – to sound calm.

"The king and queen," the boy answered.

Again, Wynn glanced up at Rhys.

"Why would you think that?" Rhys asked.

"Dad's always saying how the king and queen are going to steal his magic and take him away," the girl said. She had a magic wand in her hand that she'd been playing with before being rudely interrupted.

Wynn glanced up at Rhys for a third time.

*What do I tell them? I can't tell them their father was taken by MAKs and that they probably won't see him again for a long time – if ever. They're just kids. The boy doesn't even look like he's a teenager yet and the girl's even younger.*

"Your dad had some very important magic-related business to take care of at the castle," Rhys lied. "Is your mother around?"

"No," the little girl answered, her gaze shifting to the floor. "Mom's not around. I miss her."

Rhys and Wynn glanced at each other.

"I can tell what you're thinking," the boy said. "Mom's not dead. She's adventuring in the Northern Plains. Mom's a powerful fighter just like I'm going to be."

"I'm going to be a powerful non-binary wizard just like my dad," the girl added.

"When's your mom's adventuring party supposed to return?" Rhys asked.

The boy held up ten fingers, dropping one at a time until only three remained. He then repeated the process, going over the math one more time to double-check his work, then answered with confidence.

"Three days."

Malaric came up from behind Rhys and startled him. His knife-wielding hand came right back up as he turned around.

"Whoa, easy," Malaric said, guiding Rhys' hand down. "It's just me. What's going on? And who are they?"

"I'm Ayen," the boy replied before Rhys' had a chance to. "And this is my little sister, Farryn. She's nine and I'm twelve."

"It's nice to meet you, Ayen and Farryn," Rhys said to the kids. "Give us a minute to talk. We'll be right back."

Rhys, Wynn, and Malaric returned to the front of the store and talked quietly. Rhys explained to Malaric what the kids had told them.

"We should probably get out of here," Wynn said.

"We can't just leave those kids by themselves," Rhys replied.

"Why not? They've got a roof over their head, lots of stuff to play with..."

"I'm with Rhys," Malaric said. "They're just children. We can't leave them here by themselves."

"Fine," Wynn replied. "But *you're* taking care of them. I want no part of that shit."

The three of them once again went out back. The kids were still in the last row playing.

"Do you have any friends or relatives in town you could stay with until your mom gets back?" Rhys asked.

Ayen held up five fingers. One at a time, they all went down. He repeated the process with the other hand: same result.

"No," the boy answered. "We don't have any other family in Ostaville. And all our parents' friends are with Mom in the Northern Plains."

*Maybe we can find someone at the tavern who will watch them.*

"Who's hungry?" Rhys asked. "Do you kids want to go get some food?"

"What about Dad?" the girl asked.

"He told us he might be gone for a while and asked us to close up his shop for him. And to keep an eye on the two of you."

The kids turned to each other. Farryn whispered something to her brother, then Ayen whispered something back to her. They nodded to each other and turned to Rhys.

"Okay," Ayen said. "We'll go with you to get some food."

The kids helped show the adults how to lock up the magic shop. Then they all walked to The Bern Tavurn. It was the middle of the day and, while there were a handful of patrons in there, the tavern wasn't packed like it seemed to always be at night. They had their pick of tables and sat at one in the middle of the tavern.

"It's *that* asshole," Wynn said when he spotted Cedric behind the bar chatting with a female server. "I should go plant my warhammer between his eyes for ratting out Ena."

"Can I help?" Ayen asked.

"No," Rhys replied.

"Can I at least watch?" Ayen asked.

"Nobody's planting anything between Cedric's eyes," Rhys said.

"You're no fun," Ayen said.

"He's never any fun," Wynn replied.

"Excuse me for a minute," Rhys said, getting up from the table and walking over to the bar.

"Cedric," Rhys said, sitting down on a barstool.

"Welcome back to The Bern Tavurn," the dwarf said. "But I won't be your server today. Someone should be over to your table shortly."

"That someone is me," the woman Cedric was talking to said and walked out from behind the bar.

"That's not why I came over here," Rhys said to Cedric.

Rhys explained the situation with the children. He asked Cedric if he'd be willing to watch them for a few days until their mother returned.

"I'm sorry. I'd like to help. Really. But I have to work eighteen hours a day just to support my own family."

"Is there someone else we can leave the kids with?" Rhys asked.

"Being the progressive town Ostaville is," Cedric replied, sticking his nose up in the air, "we *do* have a childcare center."

While Rhys and Cedric were talking, Wynn wandered over to them and had a seat next to Rhys at the bar. Much to Rhys' surprise, Wynn didn't say a word. He just sat there grilling Cedric.

"Great!" Rhys said. "Where is it? Who's in charge of it?"

"I was hoping you weren't going to ask that," Cedric replied, his nose not so high anymore. He pointed across the room to a creepy looking, drunk old man sitting by himself in the corner of the tavern, drooling all over the place.

"Him?" Rhys asked.

"Old Slizy's a retired Xamosian priest. He offers childcare out of his home and has made it quite clear that any and all children are welcome at any time."

"How long has he been in business?" Rhys asked.

"Oh, many, many years."

Feeling a little more optimistic, Rhys asked, "And there haven't been any complaints?"

"Not a single one."

Feeling even more optimistic, Rhys had one last question: "And Slizy's taken care of lots of children?"

"Not a single one," Cedric answered. "For some reason, no one wants to leave their kids with him."

*Gee, I can't imagine why. Even from across the room that guy gives me the creeps.*

"I guess we'll be the first then," Wynn said, finally breaking his silence. He began waving his hand at Slizy, trying to get the man's attention. Rhys grabbed his friend's arm.

"We can't leave the kids with that guy. Look at him!" Rhys said.

"So you just want to leave them here at the tavern?" Wynn asked.

"You can't do that," Cedric said.

"That's not what I was going to suggest," Rhys replied to Cedric, then turned to Wynn. "They'll have to stay with us until the mother gets back from the Northern Plains or the dad gets released from the castle."

Both Wynn and Cedric lowered their eyebrows at him.

"It's only for a few days," Rhys added.

"They can stay with you and Malaric," Wynn said.

Rhys and Wynn rejoined Malaric and the kids at the table. Rhys told them he'd just received a message from their father saying it would be a few days until he got home and asked the adventurers to take care of them. The children were a little suspicious at first. But after a couple pieces of sugar cake each, the kids were happy to stay with them.

12.

The following morning, Wynn woke up in his empty room after a long night of drinking at the tavern. As usual, his first order of business was to go outside and relieve himself. Already up and dressed for the day, Rhys was out in front of the inn with the two kids.

"You're up awfully early. Trouble sleeping?" Wynn said and laughed as he walked around the building. A minute later, he came back around and asked, "So what are we doing today, adopting a baby dragon? Or how about an entire family of goblinoids?"

"You can't say that," an elven man said as he passed by.

"Can't say *what*?" Wynn asked, annoyed.

"In Ostaville, we don't use hate speech like that," the passerby said with a smug grin on his face. "The G-word is derogatory. We call them green-skinned forest dwellers."

"How's *this* for derogatory," Wynn said, stepping toward the elven man. He reached behind his back to grab his warhammer. But it – along with all his gear – was in his room. "You're lucky I don't have my warhammer or I'd smash that smug look off your face."

"And that's why *all* weapons should be banned," the elf replied, still smug-mugging at Wynn.

"What about *this* weapon?" Wynn asked. He raised a fist and started walking toward the man quickly, raising the other along the way. "Or *this* one?"

The elven man's grin disappeared and he scampered off down the road. Malaric came out of his room and joined the others in front of the inn.

"What are we doing today?" Malaric asked.

"I'm hungry," Ayen said.

"Me too," Farryn agreed.

"How about this," Rhys suggested. "We'll all go get some breakfast at the tavern. Then we'll split up into groups until the afternoon."

"Works for me," Wynn said. "I want to pay a visit to the weaponsmith to see his goods."

"Can I go with you?" Ayen asked.

Wynn looked down at the boy, giving him the silent, evil eye. Rhys and Malaric both knew what it meant, but Ayen didn't seem to. Or maybe he did but just wasn't afraid of Wynn.

"Pleeeaaase?" Ayen asked. "I love weapons. I want to be a big, strong fighter just like you when I'm old enough to start adventuring."

"Wouldn't you rather go to the bakery with me and your sister?" Rhys suggested, thinking for sure the boy would agree. "We'll be getting there right around the time they should be putting out the day's sweets and treats!"

"No," Ayen replied bluntly to Rhys. The boy again looked up at Wynn and asked, "Pleeeaaase?"

"You'd rather look at weapons than eat freshly made candy?" Wynn asked.

"Yes," Ayen replied just as bluntly to Wynn as he had to Rhys.

Wynn again gave Ayen the evil eye. The boy didn't budge.

"Okay, fine," Wynn reluctantly agreed. "You can come with me to the weapon shop."

They all went to the tavern for breakfast –
after Wynn had gotten fully dressed, of course. As
planned, they broke up into three groups once
everyone finished eating. Rhys took Farryn to the
bakery and Malaric wandered around Ostaville by
himself. That just left Wynn and Ayen. The twelve-
year-old boy proudly led Wynn to the weaponsmith.
It was one of Ayen's favorite places in all of Ostaville
and he went there with his mother whenever she'd let
him. Along the way, Ayen asked Wynn a series of
questions. Normally, Wynn didn't like being asked a
lot of questions – or *any* questions for that matter. But
the questions Ayen asked were the kind Wynn was
more than happy to answer:

"What's the bloodiest battle you've ever been
in?"

"How many skulls have you crushed with
your warhammer?"

"Who do you think would win in a fight: a
berserker under a powerful spell or a powerful
spellcaster going berserk?"

Wynn had to ponder that last one for a minute.
Just as he was about to answer, they got to the
weapon shop. Ayen opened the door and walked right
in as if he owned the place. Wynn followed. The air
inside the large building was much warmer than the
cool outside air. In the front of the shop, weapons of
all shapes and sizes hung from the walls. Far behind
the counter but in the same room – the whole place
was all one big room – the weaponsmith and his
apprentice were working.

*Cling! Cling! Cling!*

The weaponsmith swung a large hammer over
and over at a piece of glowing-red metal his

apprentice held in place over an anvil. Wynn couldn't help but be impressed by the man's size. The weaponsmith's arms, chest – everything, really – were massive. That tended to happen after decades of twelve-hour hammer-swinging days. After one final swing, the hardest yet, the weaponsmith put the hammer down and walked over to the counter. He instantly recognized Ayen.

"I know your mother's still out adventuring, but where's your father?"

"Ayen" Wynn said, "go play with one of those swords or something while I talk to the weaponsmith."

The boy didn't need to be told twice. He ran over and pulled a shortsword down off the wall. While Ayen played with the deadly weapon, Wynn explained the situation to the shop owner. He told him about what'd happened to Ayen's father and about how Rhys decided they should watch the kids until their mother returned from the Northern Plains.

"Unless *you* want to watch them," Wynn suggested.

"Ayen's a good kid. His sister is, too, though I don't see nearly as much of her as I do him. But I'm too busy to keep an eye on them. Even if I wasn't, a weapon shop is no place for children to be hanging around. Wynn noticed that the weaponsmith hadn't looked him in the eyes once. He was watching Ayen the whole time. Wynn turned around to see what the weaponsmith was staring at.

"Ya!" Ayen grunted as he swung the shortsword, using both hands to wield the weapon. "Huh!" he groaned as he lunged forward in a stabbing motion.

"Where'd you learn how to swing a sword like that, kid?" Wynn asked.

"My mom has been teaching me when she's home in between adventurers. But she's been going out more and more because our family needs the money."

"What for?"

"Taxes, I think," Ayen replied, having to think about it for a second. "Her and Dad are always talking about how they keep going up to pay for all the MAKs and everything."

"Well, you've got some serious skills. And you're more aggressive than most grownup fighters. Certainly more than the other fighter I'm with. Attack me," Wynn said, grabbing a shortsword off the wall.

"Hey!" the weaponsmith yelled. "You can't-"

"Relax. I'll pay for the swords if anything gets broken," Wynn said to the shop owner, then turned to Ayen. "Come on. Attack me. Give me all you've got."

Ayen looked at the weaponsmith. He shook his head.

"What are you, afraid?" Wynn taunted.

"No."

"Cause *real* fighters are never scared. I ain't afraid of nothin'."

Again, Ayen looked to the shop owner for guidance. And again, he just shook his head.

"But if you're too much of a scared little chicken-"

"I'm not scared!" Ayen yelled and charged at Wynn.

The boy swung his shortsword at Wynn over and over. The experienced fighter easily blocked every attempt.

"Is that all ya got?" Wynn taunted further.

Ayen came at Wynn even harder, slashing and stabbing at him repeatedly. Though Wynn was still able to block each attack, he did so with slightly less ease.

"That's a little better," Wynn said. "But I still don't see the fire in your eyes."

"Arrrggghhh!" the boy yelled and swung harder than ever.

*Cling!*

Wynn raised his shortsword and blocked the attack. Ayen's cracked, a few small pieces of metal splintering off. The boy knelt before Wynn, turned the broken sword around, and offered him the hilt.

"I lost," Ayen said, struggling to look up at Wynn when his eyes desperately wanted to look anywhere else. "You defeated me."

"Actually," Wynn said, offering the boy a hand and pulling him up to his feet, "*you* won. Because you weren't fighting *me* – you were fighting *yourself*. A true warrior's battle is not with his enemy, but with his own anxiety and apprehension. On the battlefield, you must be totally focused and can't let anything stand in the way of that aggression."

"So I did good?" Ayen asked, still a bit unsure.

"You did great, kid," Wynn replied, playfully rubbing the top of the boy's head, further messing up his already unkempt hair. Despite his best efforts, Ayen couldn't hide his massive smile.

"You're going to have to pay for that broken shortsword," the weaponsmith said.

"No shit," Wynn replied. "I already told you I would. And I'm going to pay for *this one*, too."

"But you didn't damage that one."

"Again: no shit. You want the sale or not?"

"Of course," the shop owner replied. "That'll be ten gold for each sword. So twenty in total."

"And I'll need a scabbard," Wynn added.

"That'll be one additional gold," the weaponsmith said and handed him a scabbard from behind the counter.

Wynn handed the man two platinum pieces and one gold, thanked him, and left the weapon shop with Ayen right behind him.

As they walked, Ayen asked Wynn, "Why did you buy a shortsword with a scabbard when you've already got a warhammer and a knife?"

"They're not for me," Wynn replied.

He stopped in the middle of the road, leaned down, and handed the sheathed sword to Ayen. The boy's face lit up like a torch for a second, then quickly extinguished.

"As much as I-" Ayen said. "My family can't afford to pay for-"

"You and your family don't owe me anything," Wynn interrupted. "Consider it a gift – at least the second one you've been given."

"What do you mean *second*?"

"You're a natural when it comes to fighting," Wynn explained. "You've got a real talent for it – a gift from Xamos. I've met some worthless, clumsy-ass fighters who have no business holding a weapon in their hands. But you – you could be a famous warrior someday if you develop your talent. And that's why I bought you the sword. You're talented, but you need practice."

"Thank you," Ayen said, his face lighting up once again. "Thank you!"

The boy first tried putting the scabbard around his waist. Ayen was tall for a twelve-year old, but not quite tall enough – the tip of the scabbard dragged along the ground as he walked. So he took it off his waist and slung the scabbard over his shoulder. There, it fit comfortably.

Wynn and Ayen walked around Ostaville for a while. An ear-to-ear smile stayed on the boy's face the entire time. Ayen wore the shortsword proudly, reaching behind his back every so often as if to make sure it was still there. Eventually it became time to meet up with the others in front of the inn.

"Where'd Ayen get the sword?" Rhys asked immediately, clearly unhappy about it.

"Where'd Farryn get the candy?" Wynn replied, pointing to a small pouch the girl had.

"You know where she got it. I bought it for her this morning."

"Well, I bought the sword for *him* this morning. So don't even think about trying to high-road me on this one."

"Candy and a sword are not the same thing and you know it!" Rhys said. "Do you really think it's appropriate to buy a child a deadly weapon?"

"I wasn't going to bring it up," Wynn replied. "But since *you* just did: Yes, I think it's appropriate to buy a boy something to defend himself and his sister with since his father is going to be-"

"Who's hungry?" Rhys interrupted, changing the subject. Everyone was except for Farryn. She'd been eating candy all day and even had a mouthful at that moment. "Let's go to the tavern and stuff our faces until we feel like we're going to explode."

After eating a huge meal at The Bern Tavurn, the group went back to the inn for the night.

"Hey Wynn," Ayen asked. "Can I stay in your room?"

"Don't you want to stay in the same room as your sister?" Rhys replied.

Rhys knew Wynn well enough to know he greatly preferred sleeping alone. But Farryn didn't.

"It's okay," she said. "I don't mind if Ayen's just going to be next door."

"Pleeeaaase?" Ayen begged. "That way you can tell me some more stories about the adventures you've been on and all the enemies you've smashed."

"Fine," Wynn reluctantly agreed. The man *did* love telling stories about smashing enemies. "But if you snore and it wakes me up in the middle of the night, I'm kicking you out."

13.

The next morning they all met up outside the inn. Ayen made it through the night in Wynn's room without getting kicked out. However, Wynn did wake up Ayen with *his* snoring once or twice. But the boy easily fell right back asleep, his new shortsword by his side.

The adventurers were eager to get through the day. That night would bring the double-full moon. Braylin had told them she'd be in contact that evening with the plan for the following day. Just as Braylin and Sandor predicted, Ena – along with a few others – were scheduled to be hanged in the town center. It's all anyone in Ostaville were talking about it. There were even a few pieces of parchment posted around town promoting the event. One posted in front of the inn read:

*You won't want to miss this season's hangings. Be the first to see a wizard get hanged for using fire magic!*

All races are welcome at this family friendly event. There will be games, prizes, and more. You can even get a portrait drawn with the condemned.

Adults: 2 copper pieces

Children over 9: 1 copper piece

Kids 9 and under: free!

The festivities will begin mid-morning in the town center the day after the double-full moon. Hangings will be held when the sun is at its high point. Space is limited. First come, first serve.

In small, barely readable lettering at the bottom of the parchment was written:

*This quarter's executions are sponsored by*

*Panelo's Potions and ANTIMA. Sanctioned by Duke Youngvalor under the authority of His and Her Royal Majesties of Ravnia.*

The adventurers decided to break up into the same groups they had the day before. Rhys suggested they meet at the tavern for dinner a little earlier than usual. That way they could get back to the inn and wait to be contacted. Everyone agreed and went their separate ways.

Malaric spent much of the morning aimlessly wandering around Ostaville, trying to build up the courage to visit a healer he'd heard about. Although everything Malaric had heard indicated she only practiced the healing arts, everyone referred to her as a non-binary wizard. He went back and forth with himself over whether or not to go.

*What am I so afraid of? This is what I want. I finally have a chance to make it real. So why am I having such a hard time with this? Maybe I'm overthinking things. Maybe I need to just do it. Stop thinking, start doing. I'm going to do it. I'm going to go.*

Malaric turned around and walked with purpose toward the part of town where he'd heard the healer lived. It was a fairly long walk, long enough for Malaric to stop and second-guess – as well as third-and-forth guess – himself. But he ultimately decided to keep going and eventually came to the healer's home at the end of a long road.

The house was one of the nicest Malaric had ever seen. He could tell it'd been recently built not only by the way it looked, but because there were still leftover pieces of wood, stone, and other building materials in the yard. Beautiful stained-glass windows were on the front and sides of the two-story home. Smoke billowed out of the chimney, so Malaric knew someone was home. He walked up to the front door which had intricate designs carved into it, adding further to the house's overall aesthetic. The healer was obviously doing well for herself because the house must've cost a fortune. With sweaty palms, Malaric raised his hand to knock on the door – but didn't.

Do I really want to do this right now? I can still change my mind. It's not too late. I can always come here some other time. I don't have to do it now. Maybe I should wait. That'd probably be best. I think I'll come back some other time. At least now I know where she lives. I'll come back another day.

Malaric changed his mind once again – this time for good. His hand lowered and he breathed a sigh of relief. But before Malaric turned around and walked away, the front door opened.

"Good timing," an elven woman said to him.

She held the front door open and a dwarven woman walked out of the house. Along with her came a strong odor that reminded Malaric of every magic shop he'd ever been in. Caught off guard, Malaric stepped aside to let the dwarf pass but didn't say a word.

"Don't worry," the dwarven woman said to Malaric, as if she could see the word *apprehensive* written on his forehead. "You're in good hands. Venlynn's the best."

Malaric flashed a half-smile at the dwarf as she walked off. Venlynn held the door open.

"Please," she said. "Come in."

Still without saying a word, Malaric entered the house. It looked even bigger from the inside than it did from the yard. He stood in a large room with a staircase going up to the second floor on one side and a hallway leading to other rooms on the opposite side. A long wooden table with several chairs around it sat in the center of the room. Shelves lined the walls: some with books, some with herbs, and some with other magic-related items. The fireplace glowed, a medium-sized kettle hanging from a hook over the fire. Malaric looked around the room in awe, particularly dazzled by the way the colored light coming through the windows danced along the floor. Venlynn closed the front door and offered him some tea. His palms now sweatier than ever, Malaric nodded. She took the kettle off the fire and poured them each a cup.

"Here you go," Venlynn said, handing Malaric his.

"Thank you," he said and took it with unsteady hands.

"You're welcome," she replied and smiled. "Please, sit down."

Malaric took a seat at the table and Venlynn sat down next to him. In some ways she reminded him of Ena – and it wasn't because Malaric thought all elves looked alike. Venlynn stood at about the same height as his captured friend and had the same dark skin tone. Even their voices were similar. But unlike Ena who was twenty-eight years old – the equivalent of being about twenty for a human – Venlynn was much older, at least twice Ena's age. Though far from being an elderly elf, strands of silver hair were starting to come in here and there. But overall, Venlynn had a youthful glow to her that Malaric found quite attractive. And her calm demeanor put him at ease – somewhat.

"So, tell me: What can I do for you?" Venlynn asked. "I assume you're here because you've heard about me and the services I provide."

"That's right," Malaric replied, his finger anxiously circling the top of his teacup over and over. "My name is Malaric and I was born human – as you can see – but I identify as a halfling."

"Well, you've definitely come to the right place, Malaric," she said, blowing the steam from the top of her teacup. "Malaric: that sounds like a halfling name."

"It is. Malaric isn't my birth name. But I've been using it for the past couple years since I realized – since I thought I might be a halfling."

"Do you *feel* like a halfling?"

"Yes, I do. On the inside. I think."

"Then that's all that matters," Venlynn said. "If you feel like a halfling, you're a halfling. It doesn't matter what you look like on the outside, your height, how hairy your knuckles and toes are or aren't: none of that matters. It's what's on the inside that counts."

"I think so, too," Malaric replied.

"*However*, we all want the way we look on the outside to reflect how we feel on the inside. That's where I come in. And if I'm not mistaken, it's why you've come to see me today: you want me to perform a racial-reassignment spell on you. Am I right?"

"Yes, that *is* why I came here today but I'm not sure about-"

"What if I told you I wasn't born an elf?" Venlynn interrupted. "Would you believe I was born human just like you?"

"Really? I never would've guessed."

"That's because I've perfected the process to the point where it's impossible to tell the difference between someone born a particular race and someone reassigned to that race. I shouldn't say anything," Venlynn said, then lowered her voice as if she was telling a secret in the middle of a crowded tavern, "but you know the dwarven woman who left just as you came in?"

"Yes."

"She looked like a dwarf, like she'd been one her entire life, right?"

"Yes."

"Two months ago," Venlynn whispered, holding a hand up to the side of her mouth, "she was one-third orc, one-third human, and one-third vrungel."

*Vrungel? What in the world is that? I've never even heard of a such a race before.*

"Now," Venlynn continued, her voice returning to normal, "she's one-hundred-percent dwarf – as long as she keeps taking her herbs. That's why she came by this morning: to buy more herbs."

"About that. How exactly does this all work? The person who told me about you said there's a one-time spell and then herbs have to be taken regularly. Is that all there is to it?"

"Pretty much, yeah," Venlynn answered. "First, I'll cast a proprietary spell on you. It's a long one, so you'll want to get comfortable. After I finish the spell, you'll no longer look human – you'll look like a halfling. But the change is purely cosmetic. You'll still have human blood pumping through your body. That's where the herbs come in. You'll take your first dose right after I finish the spell. Then, you have to take them several times a week."

"For how long?"

"This whole process is still very new, so it's impossible to say. I have a theory that if you take the herbs long enough, eventually your heart will turn into a halfling heart and begin pumping halfling blood on its own. If I'm right, you'll no longer need them once that happens."

"How will I know when that happens – *if* it happens?"

"You won't," Venlynn replied. "There's really no way to tell. So you'll need to keep taking the herbs forever."

"And if I stop?"

"Oh, I wouldn't recommend that. You'll want to keep taking them. There's no way to know what would happen if you just stopped taking them. Probably nothing. But why risk it, right? Do you have any more questions?"

"Actually, I was wondering-"

"I already know what you're going to ask," Venlynn interrupted, looking Malaric up and down. "Don't worry. For someone who can afford such nice clothing and equipment, my services and the herbs are quite affordable."

"That's not what I was going to – Now that you mention it, how much does the spell and herbs cost?"

"The spell is one-hundred gold."

"Oh wow," Malaric replied. "That's a lot."

"You don't have a hundred gold?" Venlynn asked, again eyeing him up and down.

"I do."

"Most people think a hundred gold is a steal. Think about what you're really buying: peace of mind, feeling comfortable in your own skin for the first time in your life. But if you don't want to be happy, if you'd rather keep living a lie-"

"No," Malaric stated. "I want to do it."

"You've made an excellent choice," Venlynn said with a smile. "All of my clients – from the eight-year-old dwarf turned half-orc to the one-hundred-and-ninety-seven-year-old elf turned half-halfling, half-gnome – have been very happy and you will be, too."

"Did you say eight? Isn't that a bit young?"

"You're never too young to be happy," Venlynn replied, dismissively. "Ready to get started?"

"Um, I think so."

"Great. You can give me ten platinum, one-hundred gold, or one-thousand silver – but I don't take copper."

Malaric handed her ten platinum pieces. Venlynn left the room and he heard her drop them into what sounded like a bucket full of other coins. She promptly returned and walked over to a bookshelf to the left of the fireplace. Going book by book, Venlynn thought out loud until she found the right volume.

"Imp to goblin, goblin to hobgoblin, goblin to human, human to dwarf, human to elf, human to gnome... Ah, here we go: human to halfling."

Venlynn pulled the volume down and opened it to a bookmarked page. Then she collected a few items from the shelves to the right of the fireplace and sat back down next to Malaric. Now, in addition to his palms, Malaric felt sweat on his forehead and neck, under his arms, and even felt a single bead slide down his butt crack. Fear and excitement pulsed through his human body – but it wouldn't be human for much longer. Venlynn began casting the lengthy spell. It was so long that, even though Malaric tried to pay close attention to every word and every gesture, he found his mind wandering from time to time.

*What if I don't like being a halfling? I can just go back to being human, right? I probably should've asked her before agreeing to this. I'm sure I'm going to love it. I've wanted this for years now. But what if Venlynn botches the spell and turns me into one of those vrungel things? That would suck... I think.*

Eventually Venlynn finished the racial-reassignment spell. Malaric didn't feel any different. She told him to go into the next room and look at himself in the large reflecting glass on the wall.

"Well?" Venlynn asked when Malaric returned.

"I... I'm blown away. I love it – mostly."

"What *don't* you love?"

"I'm still the same height," he said. "I thought I'd be shorter. I've never met a halfling this tall."

"Ah, yes. I was surprised you didn't mention wanting to be shorter."

"I thought that was implied. Can you make me shorter?"

"I can, yes," Venlynn answered. "But that'll be another ten gold."

Malaric reluctantly gave her a platinum piece and she cast another spell on him. It was much shorter, over in less than a minute. This time, Malaric *did* feel different. He got up to go look in the reflecting glass again. When he did, his breeches fell to the floor. A little embarrassed, Malaric had to hold them up as he walked into the next room.

*Wow*, he thought, looking at his reflection. *Just wow.*

Malaric had entered Venlynn's home a six-foot-tall human. But now staring back at him stood a three-and-a-half-foot-tall halfling. Any embarrassment Malaric had felt disappeared. He let his breeches fall to the floor and stepped out of them, then took off his now-oversized tunic. Malaric began twisting and turning in front of the glass to examine every inch of his body. There wasn't even a hint of his former-human self. From Malaric's head to his now-hairy toes – and *everywhere* in between – he'd become a halfling. Malaric's outer transformation was complete.

"Well?" Venlynn asked.

"I love it," Malaric replied, putting his ill-fitting clothes back on and returning to the living room. "All of it. Thank you so very much. I guess I'll need to buy some new clothes."

"And some herbs," she added, placing a leather pouch filled with pungent herbs on the table. "A month's worth is five gold. But only twelve gold for three months."

Malaric bought three months worth of herbs and again thanked Venlynn. She escorted him to the door and they said goodbye. The road leading back to town seemed a lot longer now that Malaric was a lot shorter. He struggled to carry his equipment while holding up his breeches. Malaric could feel the eyes of everyone he passed along the way upon him but didn't care. He felt too happy to let it get to him.

"Looks like someone just visited Venlynn," a woman whispered to the man walking next to her as they passed Malaric. Both giggled.

Eventually, Malaric found his way to a clothing shop and bought a new outfit to match his new halfling frame. He realized it was getting late and walked to The Bern Tavurn to meet the others. They were already seated at a table.

"Well?" Malaric asked. "What do you think?"

Wynn, after looking him up and down said, "You're not my type."

Rhys stared blankly at Malaric for a moment. Then his eyebrows raised when he noticed the halfling – though wearing a different outfit – was carrying all of his friend's belongings.

"Malaric?" Rhys asked. "Mal, is that you?"

"It sure is," the halfling replied. "What do you think?"

"Aaahahahaha!" Wynn laughed like a maniac, slamming his fist against the table several times, nearly falling out of his seat.

"What's so funny?" Malaric asked.

"Yeah," Ayen repeated. "What's so funny?"

"Nothing," Wynn replied, trying – and failing – to calm himself. "Nothing at all. Not a thing."

Malaric joined his friends at the table – eventually. Still getting used to his new height, he struggled to get up on a chair. Wynn chortled.

After the early dinner, they all went to the inn to wait for Braylin. She showed up with a couple other Rising Shadow members just as the sun went over the horizon, all of them wearing hooded robes to hide their identities. After first explaining who the halfling was and then who the kids were, Rhys asked Braylin about the plan for the following day.

"Ah yes, the plan," she said, lowering her voice. "As I'm sure you're well aware by now, at high noon tomorrow your friend – along with a few other unfortunate souls – are to be hanged in the center of town. But if all goes according to plan, that's not going to happen. Here's what we're going to do..."

14.

The next morning, Rhys, Malaric, and Wynn got into position, hiding in the bushes along the road going directly from the duke's castle to the center of town. They were waiting to ambush the MAKs as they transported the condemned. The kids were told to stay in Rhys' room at the inn until someone returned for them. Though they really didn't want to miss the social event of the season, the children reluctantly agreed to stay put.

"I don't get it," Rhys said, his muscles tense, partly due to the weather. It was the coldest and windiest it'd been since getting to Ostaville. "They should've been here by now."

"I don't get it either," Malaric replied.

At the same time, all three of them heard someone running up the road.

"Get down," Rhys whisper-yelled. "That might be them."

It wasn't.

The runner stopped in the middle of the road not far from where they hid. Peeking out from behind the bushes, Rhys recognized the runner as one of the Rising Shadow members with Braylin the night before.

"They're already," the man shouted between gasps, trying to catch his breath. "In the center. Of town. They took. An alternate route."

Rhys, Wynn, and Malaric emerged from behind the bushes on one side of the road. Braylin, Iolas, and two other Rising Shadow members joined them, coming out from behind the bushes on the other side.

"What?" Braylin said. "How can that be? They always use this road. Always."

"I have no idea," the runner said, still panting but able to speak in complete sentences. "Maybe somebody tipped them off that we'd be waiting for them."

"What are we going to do?" Iolas asked Braylin. "Our whole plan is ruined."

"We've got to try to stop them," Rhys said and took off down the road toward the center of town. "We have to save Ena!"

Without hesitation, Wynn bolted down the road after Rhys, just a few paces behind his friend. Malaric followed immediately after. However, the halfling found it impossible to keep up with the two humans.

"Come on!" Braylin yelled a second later, motioning for the other Rising Shadow members to follow.

Rhys and Wynn were the first to arrive at the town center. The others caught up soon after, Malaric being the last. A massive crowd had gathered. Members of every race, including children of all ages, packed the center of town. But it wasn't the crowd that had Rhys' stomach twisting in knots – it was what the crowd had come to see.

In the middle of the town center, a long, wooden stage had been erected. It stood several feet off the ground. And on the stage, gallows had been set up. Five nooses hung from the gallows, each tied around someone's neck. Rhys and Wynn recognized two of them immediately: Ena and Yorlumin, the magic-shop owner. Malaric was too short to see them at first, but Rhys gave him a boost so he could see the stage for himself.

"I'm going to work my way up front," Rhys said.

"I'm going with you," Wynn replied.

"Me, too," Malaric added.

"What are you going to do?" Braylin asked.

"I have no idea," Rhys answered. "Yet."

"We'll spread out and provide whatever support we can," Braylin said.

Rhys nodded, then turned and immediately began weaving his way through the crowd toward the stage. Wynn and Malaric followed. It wasn't easy and they managed to piss off several crowd members, but the three of them found their way to the front. There, they had a much better view of the stage.

Ena, the magic-shop owner, and the three other condemned all looked terrified. Each had a noose around their neck, hands tied behind their back, and stood on top of a trap door. Though none of them had bags around their heads, the executioner did. Over on the right side of the stage next to a giant lever stood what everyone could tell was a dwarven man with a sack on his head. The short and stocky stature, long braided beard, and hairy hands were a dead giveaway.

Guards were everywhere. At each corner of the stage stood two armed MAKs wearing heavy, full-plate armor. Behind the stage, they could see five horses they assumed had been used to transport the prisoners to the gallows and would likely be used to transport their corpses away. Talking to the executioner on the stage stood a MAK who's back had been turned to the crowd. When he turned around a minute later, they recognized him as Sir Adeleath, the MAK who'd taken Ena from the tavern. His full-plate helmet was on, but with the face shield up they could see his face.

Ena spotted Rhys and Wynn in the crowd, but couldn't see Malaric. Even if she could've, she wouldn't have recognized him. When Rhys noticed Ena looking at him, they locked eyes. He'd never seen his friend so scared. By the look of it, she'd been crying – and so had several of the others on the stage. It made Rhys want to take out his longsword and start chopping heads. But Rhys was smart enough to know that, even if he managed to chop a head or two, it wouldn't be long before it would be his own getting hacked off.

"I see nine MAKs altogether," Wynn said. "There's no way we can defeat them all, not to mention the crowd if any of them get involved."

"Well, we have to do something," Rhys replied, glancing up. "The sun will be reaching its high point soon."

"I have an idea," Malaric said. "Time to put my old rogue skills to good use."

"Where are you-" Rhys asked as Malaric stepped away from them.

"Wait for my mark," Malaric interrupted. "Don't do anything until then."

"What mark?" Wynn asked. "What the hell are you-"

Using his small stature to his advantage, Malaric disappeared, easily weaving his way through the crowd. Sir Adeleath shook the executioner's hand and approached the front of the stage. As he did, the crowd's incessant chatter gradually softened until only a few whispers could be heard here and there.

*What is Malaric doing?* Rhys wondered, glancing at the sky. A few clouds had rolled in, but he could still see the sun almost directly overhead. *We have to do something and soon. It looks like they're about to start the execution ceremony.*

Rhys was right. Adeleath clapped his hands and the chatter stopped. All eyes were up front. The knight shut his face shield, then removed his helmet and held it under his arm.

"We are gathered here today," Sir Adeleath said, "to witness the hanging of five criminals and enemies of not only Duke Youngvalor, but also of His and Her Royal Majesties of Ravnia. Each of the wicked souls you see behind me have committed at least one serious infraction against the good people of Ostaville. And every one of those infractions involved the use, sale, or promotion of fire magic."

Several people in the crowd gasped, even though everyone in Ostaville knew why the executions were taking place. Rhys looked up at the sky again. The sun was now entirely hidden behind a thick layer of dense clouds.

"By the power vested in me by Duke Youngvalor," Adeleath continued, "and to him by the king and queen of Ravnia, I hereby use my vested power to vest power in our anonymous executioner, so that he may pull the lever with the blessings of myself, the duke, the king and queen, and of Xamos himself.

"For those of you who are here for your first execution: welcome. You picked one that will likely be remembered for generations. On my mark, our honorable executioner will pull the lever, releasing the trap door each of the condemned are standing on. When they fall through the floor, their souls will be released so they may stand before the mighty Xamos himself, to be judged for all eternity."

Rhys had never felt so utterly hopeless in his entire life. He once again looked to the sky, this time to beg Xamos for his mercy when dealing with Ena.

*If you must take my friend, if you must take all five of those poor souls, please let their deaths be quick and painless. And please treat their souls as mercifully as you would a young child. I beg you all-powerful Xamos, ruler of above, below, and everything in between. Please be-*

Normally, Rhys would never be so disrespectful as to end a prayer mid-sentence. He believed Xamos to be just as cruel, vengeful, and petty as he could be kind, compassionate, and merciful. It didn't make a whole lot of sense to Rhys, but he didn't question it. There weren't many things that could stop Rhys mid-prayer, but this was one of them.

"Snow," he whispered.

"What?" Wynn asked. "What'd you just say?"

"Wynn, look," Rhys replied, pointing up at the sky. At first, he spotted a single snowflake. Then another and another. "I told you it was real!"

"The hell are you talking about, Rhys? I don't see any-" Then Wynn swallowed hard and his lips parted. He *did* see it. Wynn was so shocked that only a single word slipped from his mouth: "Fuuuck."

What started as just a few snowflakes quickly turned into dozens, then hundreds. It wasn't long before other members of the crowd noticed.

"Look!" someone yelled. "Look at the sky!"

More than a few people gasped. "Oohs," "aahs," and a variety of other sounds came from all around the crowd. Before long, there was so much chatter that Rhys couldn't hear Adeleath's voice, even from his spot near the stage. With the snow picking up rapidly and the crowd growing louder by the second, Adeleath quickly became frustrated. A thin layer of snow accumulated on his head. The MAK stopped talking and glanced up at the sky. Then Adeleath put his helmet back on and turned to the executioner.

"Now!" he shouted, using both hands to make a lever-pulling motion.

"Noooooo!" Rhys yelled.

The executioner wrapped both of his hairy, muscular hands around the lever and pulled it with all his strength. Rhys could barely watch, expecting to see the floor fall out from underneath the five victims, but couldn't bring himself to look away.

Nothing happened.

"What the?" the executioner mumbled, then re-wrapped his hands around the lever even tighter. Again he pulled, this time yanking it.

Again: nothing.

*What in the name of Xamos is going on? Did you answer my prayer? Is this because of you?*

Rhys didn't know it yet, but the malfunctioning lever had less to do with divine intervention and more to do with his small-statured friend. Snow now filled the sky and had begun accumulating on the stage. Everyone in the crowd looked up, pointing and talking about the strange phenomenon. Someone to Rhys' left caught his attention.

"Look at that!" an half-elven woman yelled, pointing directly above Adeleath.

Hovering a few feet above the MAK's head was a thick sheet of ice. When Rhys first noticed it, the ice was just floating there – but not for long.

*Crash!!!*

The massive block of ice fell directly on top of Adeleath, knocking him down. A few members of the crowd who saw it happen screamed at the top of their lungs. This caused several more to scream, sending a rippling effect through the crowd. Everyone panicked and started to disperse. People ran in every direction – or at least tried to. A thin coating of snow covered the ground, making it very slippery. Unaccustomed to running in snow – or doing anything in it, really – members of the crowd struggled to stay upright, slipping and sliding all over the place.

*It must be Braylin and the others. Sheets of ice don't just appear out of nowhere and start falling on knights for no reason. Magic's the only way ice can be created. It MUST be them.*

"That's our cue!" Rhys yelled to Wynn and reached for his longsword.

"Way ahead of you, buddy," Wynn replied, his warhammer already in hand.

Rhys and Wynn charged at the two MAKs closest to them, the ones standing next to the front-left corner of the stage. The dense crowd that had been between them and the MAKs ran off leaving a clear path. But even though there were no people in the way, the path was anything but clear. The snow was now falling so quickly, Rhys and Wynn could only see a foot or two in front of them. And if the near-whiteout conditions made movement difficult, the slippery snow-covered ground made it almost impossible.

*Cling! Clang!*

Rhys got to the MAKs a moment before Wynn – who'd slipped in the snow – and immediately attacked. He swung his longsword overhead at one of the MAKs, who blocked it with his own longsword. Right away the MAK countered, but Rhys managed to deflect the blow with his wooden shield. Wynn recovered from his fall quickly and got to the MAKs a moment later. The fall made him angry and Wynn took it out on the MAK closest to him, swinging his warhammer as hard as he could.

*Whiff!*

Nothing but air. The MAK stepped back just in time to avoid what would've been a devastating blow to the head. Fortunately for Wynn, the MAK was too busy trying to regain his balance after stepping back and sliding in the snow to counter attack. It likely would've been an easy kill shot because when Wynn swung his warhammer and missed, it completely threw him off balance and he fell backward landing on his butt again. But Wynn quickly got back up to his feet and continued battling the two MAKs with Rhys.

Between the chaos and poor visibility, Malaric had managed to climb up onto the stage – which stood almost as tall as him – without being seen. After taking out a dagger, Malaric used his stealth skill to sneak up behind the executioner. Although, the man was so distracted Malaric could've approached him from the front *without* using stealth and he still probably wouldn't've noticed. The dwarf was preoccupied with trying to figure out why the lever didn't work. He'd tug on it, let go, step back for a moment, then step forward and try again. This process repeated itself over and over.

Malaric got close enough to the executioner to use another of his old rogue skills: the backstab. Though not as effective as the double-backstab – precisely *half* as effective – it would have to do. Just as the executioner was about to grab the lever for the tenth time, the halfling leapt, plunging his dagger deep into the dwarf's back.

"Uggghhh," the executioner – now executionee – yelled.

The dwarf fell to the stage face first with Malaric on top of him. The halfling pulled his dagger out of the man's back. Though he'd stopped moving, Malaric wanted to make sure the executioner had actually been executed. So he used the bloody dagger to slit the dwarf's throat. The cut sliced open not only the executioner's throat – it also sliced open the sack over his head. Though Malaric didn't expect to know who the man was, he peeled the sack open to reveal the dwarf's face.

"Unbelievable," Malaric said under his breath when he saw who it was.

The halfling didn't waste any time dwelling on it. He quickly hopped up and rushed over to Ena. Between Malaric's natural dexterity and the fact that his halfling body had a much lower center of gravity than his human and elven counterparts, it was much easier for him to walk on the snow. However, it was also his short stature that made it impossible to cut the noose around Ena's neck. Malaric had sheathed the dagger and tried to use his serrated knife to cut it, but couldn't reach up that high. But he *could* reach the rope tying Ena's hands behind her back.

"Thank you, kind sir," Ena said, her hands now free.

"Here," the halfling replied, handing her the knife. While Ena used it to cut the noose, he continued, "Thank me later if you, me, Rhys, and Wynn somehow make it out of here in one piece."

"Do I know you?" Ena asked, looking at Malaric curiously as she finished cutting through the noose. Ena went to hand him back the knife.

"Use it to help me free the others," he said, unsheathing the still-bloody dagger. "You cut the nooses, I'll get their hands."

"But I don't know who-"

"I'll explain later," Malaric shouted. "Go!"

One by one, Ena and Malaric went down the line freeing each of the prisoners. The two MAKs that had been guarding the back-right stage area saw them – just barely through the blizzard-like conditions – and carefully walked up the wooden stairs to stop them. As Ena and Malaric freed the fifth and final prisoner, the MAKs closed in on them. They both knew they were in trouble. With only the knife in Ena's hand and a dagger Malaric's, they were at a serious disadvantage against the fully armored, longsword-wielding MAKs. Adeleath was on the stage, too, but didn't pose a threat at the moment. Still dazed from the sheet of ice hitting him, he was struggling just to get to his feet.

The two MAKs approached Ena and Malaric with their swords overhead. The one closest to Ena prepared to swing. She held the knife – tiny in comparison to the MAK's longsword – in front of herself with two hands as if it had any chance of defending an attack. Though the MAK wore full-plate armor and a matching helmet, the face guard was up. The man flashed a sinister grin at Ena, then swung his sword at her neck, hard as he could. Though Ena had been an experienced adventurer, she was a wizard, not a fighter, and wasn't used to this type of confrontation. As a result, Ena flinched and blinked for a fraction of a second – but that was as long as it took.

"What in the..." she mumbled when her eyes reopened.

An arrow stuck out of the MAK's right eye, blood pouring from it, and his longsword was nowhere to be seen. The arrow had struck him mid-swing and the sword flew off into where the large crowd had been just minutes earlier. Right in front of Ena, the MAK fell first to his knees, then to his face.

The other MAK who'd gotten on the stage took aim at Malaric with his longsword. Only slightly better armed than Ena, the halfling held out his dagger. But unlike her, he didn't flinch or blink.

Malaric saw everything. In fact, he saw what was going to happen before the MAK knew anything bad was about to happen to him at all.

*Slam!*

Like the one that'd appeared over Adeleath's head, a massive brick of solid ice formed above the MAK's. This one was even bigger and slightly higher up. As the MAK prepared to swing at Malaric, the frozen block fell on top of him. It was so heavy that it sent the MAK crashing through the wooden stage to the ground, crushing him.

Down in front of the stage, Rhys and Wynn were still going at it with the MAKs. Two on two, they were fairly evenly matched. But the two MAKs that had been guarding to the right of the stage carefully made their way over to assist the others. Four MAKs against Rhys and Wynn wasn't so even.

"Argh," Rhys yelled as one of the MAKs sliced his sword-wielding hand open.

He tried to counter, but the MAK was easily able to defend. A different MAK attacked Wynn. He swung low, his sword slashing Wynn's ankle. It was all he could do to not fall over, so Wynn couldn't even try to attempt a counter-attack. Another MAK swung at Rhys. This time, he managed to narrowly dodge the MAK's sword. But the MAK next to him saw an opportunity and took it, stabbing Rhys in the arm. While Rhys was getting frustrated, his friend got angry.

"Aaaaaarrrrrrgggggg!" Wynn screamed and swung his warhammer as hard as he could at one of the MAK's chest.

He knew it was a foolish – borderline suicidal – thing to do. With that much power behind Wynn's swing, if he missed he'd surely slip and fall to the ground, leaving himself vulnerable to multiple attacks.

But he didn't miss.

*Bam!!!*

Wynn's warhammer hit its target dead center. The blow sent the MAK flying backward into one of the others, who tried to catch him. Didn't work. Both of them crashed to the ground. The MAK Wynn had hit wasn't moving. The fully armored knight just laid in the snow, his sword nearly a foot away from the hand it'd been in. The other MAK who'd fallen was still conscious, but struggled to get up. With his full-plate armor, the MAK kept slipping and sliding all over the place just like Adeleath on the stage.

Rhys tried to reproduce his friend's success with his longsword. He dropped his shield and swung the sword with two hands as hard as he could at one of the still-standing MAKs, aiming for the center of the chest.

*Cling!*

Direct hit. Unfortunately, the blow did little more than knock some wind from the MAK, who raised his longsword to counter. Another idea popped into Rhys' head and he had just enough time to go for it. Trying to reproduce Wynn's success in a different way, Rhys dropped his sword and charged at the MAK's legs while the knight's weapon was raised. Rhys wrapped his arms around one of the MAK's legs and violently yanked it up.

*Slam!*

The MAK went flying backward, landing on his full-plate ass. Like the knight next to him, he struggled to get up to his feet. Rhys quickly grabbed his sword from the ground and took aim at the last standing MAK.

"Move back!" Braylin yelled from somewhere.

Though they couldn't see Braylin through the falling snow, Rhys and Wynn could hear her. They both took several steps back. One of the MAKs managed to get back up to his feet. As soon as he did, a giant brick of ice appeared directly over his head and the MAK standing next to him. While the first one noticed the ice forming and stepped out of the way just in time, the other didn't.

*Crash!*

The massive piece of ice crushed the MAK into the ground, caving in his armor and shattering several bones – including his skull. Rhys and Wynn both took aim at the only MAK still standing. The knight managed to fend off several attacks. Then Wynn swung his warhammer up at the MAK's head. His face shield was up and Wynn's hammer caught it, sending the helmet flying off the knight's head. As soon as the MAK's helmet came off, so did his head. Rhys swung his longsword as hard as he could and chopped the MAK's head clean off.

Rhys and Wynn stepped over to the two MAKs on the ground struggling to get up. Wynn used his boot first to pin one of the MAKs to the ground, then to kick off his helmet. The man had blood all over his face. He raised his hands to protect himself against what he knew was coming, but it did little good.

*Crunch!*

Wynn caved in the MAK's face with his warhammer. The MAK Rhys stood over was smaller than the one Wynn had just killed – the smallest of the four by far. Rhys easily pinned the MAK down with his boot, who'd been sliding all over the place trying to get up. After raising his sword overhead, Rhys kicked off the knight's helmet.

"You're a-" Rhys said, unable to bring himself to drive his blade down. "I can't do it. I can't kill a woman like this."

Rhys slowly lowered his sword. The female MAK looked him in the eyes and the corners of her mouth almost moved.

Then her skull got caved in by a warhammer. *Crunch!*

Rhys shot Wynn a look. As he pulled his weapon out of the woman's crushed-in face, Wynn looked Rhys in the eyes and uttered a single word.

"Equality."

With the help of the only other two MAKs remaining, Adeleath finally managed to get to his feet. They went behind the stage, untied two horses, and got on them. Adeleath, still too dazed to ride his own horse, got behind one of the other MAKs. They rode off, retreating down the snow-covered road leading to the castle.

"Come on!" Malaric yelled.

Rhys and Wynn couldn't see Malaric through the falling snow, but could tell he was somewhere behind the stage. Walking cautiously through the now several inches of snow, they found their way around back. Malaric and Ena were with the three remaining horses, helping the former prisoners to get on their backs. Braylin, Iolas, and a couple other Rising Shadow members joined them behind the stage soon after.

"I've never been so happy to see you guys in my entire life," Ena said to Rhys and Wynn. "Where's Malaric?"

Rhys and Wynn both looked at the halfling, who was in the middle of helping a man twice his size to get on one of the horses. Once the man was up, Malaric turned to Ena.

"I'm Malaric," he said.

Ena just stared at him.

"You can explain later," Braylin said. "Right now, we all have to get to the safe house south of town – well, most of us do. Nyvernia and Olore: you know what you need to do."

The two Rising Shadow members nodded. Without hesitation they rushed off, quickly disappearing into the snowstorm.

"Rhys and Wynn," Braylin said. "You two-"

"We're on it," Rhys replied. "Wynn and I will go pick up Ayen and Farryn from the inn. Then we'll meet you at the safe house."

"Ayen and Farryn?" the magic-shop-owner-turned-political-prisoner-turned-rescuee asked from atop one of the horses. "Those are my children!"

"I'll explain when we all get to the safe house," Rhys replied. "Don't worry: your kids are fine. But we have to hurry."

"I almost forgot!" Malaric said and hurried over to the stage.

The halfling got down on all fours and disappeared underneath it. He reemerged a moment later, crawling back out holding a dagger between his teeth. Malaric sheathed it and rejoined the others.

Rhys and Wynn trekked through the snow on foot back to the inn. They were both bruised and bloody, leaving a trail of footprints and blood. But the snow came down so hard that the trail was covered within minutes. The others – including the former prisoners on horseback – all headed for the safe house just south of town.

15.

Hidden deep in the woods just south of Ostaville but before getting to the Seenia Mountains stood a large, snow-covered log cabin. Smoke began billowing out of its chimney as they got a fire going. Malaric, Ena, Braylin, Iolas, Yorlumin, and the three other former prisoners made it to the cabin safely. They joined Sandor who was already there and eagerly waited for Wynn, Rhys, and the two kids to arrive.

*Knock. Knock, knock, knock. Knock. Knock, knock.*

"What the hell are you doing?"

Everyone turned to face the front door when they heard voices and knocking coming from outside. It didn't take long to figure out who it was.

"What?" Rhys replied. "I'm doing a special knock so they know it's us."

"Yeah, us or a six-foot-tall woodpecker," Wynn said. "Just use your voice like a normal person."

*Bang! Bang! Bang!*

"Hey!" Wynn yelled, slamming his fist against the door. "It's us. Open up."

*Bang. Bang. Bang.*

"Yeah," Ayen yelled, imitating Wynn. "Open up!"

Yorlumin rushed over to the door and opened it. His face lit up when he saw his children, both of them covered in snow.

"Dad!" Farryn shouted and threw her arms around her father. Ayen also gave him a hug, though it wasn't quite as enthusiastic as his sister's.

They came in and joined the others. Malaric healed Rhys and Wynn by the fireplace while Yorlumin reconnected with his children.

"I never thought I'd see either of you again," he said. "What about your mother? Where is she? Has she returned from the Northern Plains?"

"Not yet," Ayen answered.

"When she returns to Ostaville, there's not telling what they'll do to-"

"Don't worry, Yorlumin," Braylin said to the magic-shop owner. "We've made sure nothing will happen to Kae. But right now I have some questions for you and the others who were taken to the castle. I know everyone's still shaken up and exhausted, but it's important."

Yorlumin, Ena, and the other three former prisoners gathered around Braylin. Iolas and Sandor joined them.

"Did any of you see or hear anything that might help us to understand what the hell is going on in Ostaville?" Braylin asked.

"I think it's obvious what's going on," Sandor replied even though Braylin wasn't talking to him. "Just like I predicted, the fire-magic ban caused the air to cool. When you cast your ice spells, it made the air cool even more leading to snow. I was right."

"There's just one problem with your theory," Braylin said. "It started snowing *before* we cast the ice spells."

Sandor looked up and stroked his smooth chin. In spite of everything that'd happened, he somehow managed to stay both impeccably dressed and groomed, unlike the others. But Sandor was just as puzzled by Braylin's comment as everyone else.

"That's because the snow isn't being caused by the fire-magic ban *or* by ice magic," Yorlumin said. Everyone looked at him eager to hear what he had to say. Even Rhys, Wynn, and the others listened from across the room. "It's being caused by the king and queen of Ravnia."

"That's absurd!" Rhys said, getting up from the fireplace.

"Please excuse my naive friend here," Wynn said, staying seated but turning to face Yorlumin and the others. "*How* is it being caused by the king and queen. And *why*?"

"The how is obvious, isn't it?" Yorlumin replied. It wasn't. Several looked at him with blank stares. "Magic!"

"Then *why*?" Rhys asked. "It doesn't make any sense. If they knew what was causing it to snow, why would they send us up here to investigate?"

"I think I'm starting to understand what's going on," Sandor said. "The elites want all magic banned and have for some time."

"Elites?" Rhys asked.

"You know," Sandor replied, "the king and queen, the dukes of each town, the CEOs of the top magic schools-"

"CEOs?"

"Chief enchantment officers. If you keep interrupting me, I'm never going to finish."

"Sorry," Rhys replied. "Go ahead."

"After several fire outbreaks," Sandor explained, "fire magic was banned in Ostaville, then Seenia. Krasnia will undoubtedly be next. After that, it'll be ice magic – maybe *all* water magic. And what better way to get people to support an ice-magic ban than by creating scary weather and blaming it on magic? First, ice magic will be banned in Ostaville, just like fire magic. Then it'll work its way south. After that, it'll be wind and earth magic. It's just a matter of time until *all* magic is banned, from EMDs all the way-"

Rhys didn't say anything, but Sandor could tell by the puzzled look on his face he didn't know what EMDs were. Most of the others didn't seem to, either.

"Enchantments of mass destruction," Sandor elaborated. "From EMDs all the way down to the most basic of healing spells."

"No way," Rhys said after waiting a moment to make sure Sandor was done talking. "I don't believe it. I *can't* believe it."

Ena got up and walked over to the fireplace. She put her hand on Rhys' shoulder and looked him in the eyes. He noticed her finger was no longer red.

"I didn't want to believe it either," Ena said. "But it's true. Why do you think the five of us just almost got executed?"

"For breaking the rules," Rhys replied.

"I'm the only one who broke an actual, written rule – and a stupid one at that," Ena said. "The others were rounded up for nothing more than their beliefs."

"It's true," Yorlumin said. "I didn't sell anyone fire magic like the MAKs accused me of. The only thing I'm guilty of is saying that no magic should be banned."

"Same here," an elven man, one of the other former prisoners, said. "All *I* did was say I thought the king, queen, dukes, and CEOs were behind the fire-magic ban at the tavern. Cedric overheard me, told the MAKs a few tables down, and they took me away."

"Cedric won't be telling any*one* any*thing* any*more*," Malaric said. Everyone looked at him. "He's dead. Cedric was the executioner back at the gallows. I stabbed him and slit his throat."

Several of them gasped. But the looks on their faces told Malaric they were pleased by the news.

"*I* did even less," a woman and one of the other former prisoners said. "I was talking to a friend about the fire-magic ban as we waited in line at the baker's. All I said was: 'What's next, wind magic?' The next thing I knew, I was being dragged to the castle and getting thrown in the dungeon."

"Even if that's all true," Rhys said, "I still don't understand. Why would they want to take away magic?"

Wynn sighed, shook his head, and muttered, "So naive."

"You really aren't kidding about him," Sandor said to Wynn, then addressed Rhys. "Power. Control. Influence. If the elites ban all magic for the common folk, then the elites will be the only ones to wield its awesome power. They'll have even more control than they do now. It's the same reason why they're pushing to ban certain types of weapons."

"I thought it was only those crazy anti-axers and anti-sword activists who want to ban weapons," Malaric said.

"And who do you think funds not just the anti-weapons movement, but also the SJWs, ANTIMA, and of course the MAKs?" Sandor asked.

"The crown," Rhys answered with his head lowered, defeat in his voice.

"Now you're getting it," Sandor replied. "The crown and their cronies – or crownies as I like to call them."

Sandor paused for a laugh. Not even a snicker.

"There's something *I* don't understand about what just happened back at the town center," Ena said. "How come Cedric couldn't pull the lever? Every time I glanced at him, he was tugging away at the thing. Why did it fail? Why didn't the trap doors open letting me and the others fall to our deaths?"

"That was me," Malaric stated proudly. "I did it."

"Did what exactly?" Wynn asked.

"When I left you and Rhys in front of the stage, I snuck through the crowd and around to the side. There was just enough room for me to slip past the MAKs guarding the corner and slide under the stage. While under there, I jammed one of my daggers into the bottom of the lever so it wouldn't work."

*Knock, knock, knock.*

Everyone turned to the door. Wynn grabbed his warhammer and hopped up. Braylin got up, too, but looked unconcerned and motioned for Wynn to sit down. He did, but kept his warhammer in his lap. Braylin walked over to the front door and knocked on it a few times herself in a particular pattern.

*Knock, knock. Knock. Knock. Knock, knock.*

She took a step back and waited for a response.

*Knock. Knock. Knock, knock. Knock. Knock.*

Braylin smiled and opened the door. Yorlumin and his two kids jumped up when they saw Kae in the doorway. She was Yorlumin's wife and the children's mother. Like Rhys and Wynn, Kae was a fighter. She wore light chainmail armor and had what could best be described as a long shortsword – or a short longsword – strapped to her back. Next to the experienced adventurer stood a female half-elf and Rising Shadow member named Nyvernia.

"Mother!"

"Mommy!"

Ayen and Farryn ran over and gave her a big hug, which Kae gave right back to them. Yorlumin got up and walked over to the door, too. He threw his arms around his wife and, although he'd wiped them before she had a chance to notice, tears had formed in the corners of his eyes.

"I thought I'd never see you again," Yorlumin said to his wife.

"So I've heard," Kae replied. "Sounds like you had even more of an adventure than I did – and without even leaving Ostaville."

After giving Yorlumin, Kae, and their two kids a minute to reunite, everyone gathered around the living room in a large circle.

"So what do we do now?" Ena asked. "We obviously can't go back to Ostaville. And we can't report back to the king and queen. Even if we get to them before word travels back from Ostaville about what happened, they're going to find out eventually."

"That's *exactly* what we're going to do," Rhys replied.

"What?" Ena asked.

"Report back to the king and queen," Rhys answered. "I have a few things I'd like to say to them."

"If you really want to be killed that badly," Wynn offered, "I'll cave your skull in right now and save you the trip."

"Thanks, buddy," Rhys replied. "You're a true friend. I can always count on you."

"You know it!"

"But I don't have a death wish," Rhys continued. "What I have is a lifetime of being lied to and I'm going to give the king and queen a piece of my mind no matter what anyone says. So if you want to stop me, you're going to have to cave my skull in. Otherwise, I'm going."

"Then I'm going, too," Wynn replied. "I've got to see this."

"You just saved me from certain death," Ena said. "I'm in."

"You've always been supportive of me regardless of what I identify as," Malaric said to Rhys, then turned to look right at Wynn. "Even when others haven't."

Wynn didn't say anything, which surprised Malaric. It surprised Rhys and Ena, too.

"What?" Malaric continued, still staring at Wynn. "No snarky comment? No rude insult about how I'm not really a halfling?"

Wynn still didn't say anything. He just sat there staring back at Malaric blankly.

"Don't just sit there looking at me like that," Malaric said practically yelling. "Say something – anything!"

Wynn took the warhammer out of his lap and placed it on the floor. The fighter got up and slowly walked over to Malaric. Wynn was now almost twice the halfling's size and just stood there a couple inches away towering over him. Rhys could see a hint of fear in Malaric's eyes, but the halfling didn't flinch. The two just stood there staring at each other. Then Wynn did something that surprised everyone.

He offered Malaric his hand.

"I'm sorry," Wynn said.

At the same time, Rhys and Ena spoke.

"Really?"

"You're *what*?"

Malaric was the last to respond. Afraid it might be a trap, he was hesitant to take Wynn's hand.

"You are? For what?"

"If it wasn't for you and your weird little halfling fetish," Wynn explained, "Ena would be dead and so would four others. If you hadn't transformed-"

"Transitioned," Malaric corrected.

"Whatever. If you hadn't changed," Wynn continued, "you never would've been able to fit under the stage to jam that lever. Ena and the others would likely still be swinging from the gallows if it wasn't for you."

Malaric looked from Wynn's eyes down to his extended hand, then back up. The halfling inhaled a slow breath, then finally reached out and shook Wynn's hand.

"Apology accepted," Malaric said and nodded. Wynn nodded back.

"I never thought I'd see the day," Rhys said, shaking his head with a big grin on his face.

"And I never through *I'd* see the day when little white pieces of frozen rain fell from the sky," Wynn replied. "Firsts for everybody today."

While this long-awaited moment took place in the middle of the room, Braylin, Iolas, Nyvernia, and Sandor talked privately over in the corner. When they finished their conversation, Braylin turned to the others.

"We'll join you," she said.

"Join who, where?" Rhys asked.

"We'll come with you to Krasnia," Braylin replied. "You're going to need all the help you can get."

Rhys knew Braylin was right. Gratefully, he accepted.

"What about us?" Farryn asked, looking up at her dad.

"Yeah," Ayen added, looking up at his mom. "What are *we* going to do?"

"Well, we can't go back to-," Kae started to answer, then noticed what was on her son's back. "Ayen, where'd you get that sword from?"

Not wanting to get Wynn in trouble, Ayen glanced over at him before answering. Wynn nodded, giving Ayen the go-ahead.

"Wynn bought it for me," the boy stated, proudly. "He says I'm a natural and has been teaching me some moves. You want to see?"

"Yes, I do. But not right now," Kae replied, then picked up where she'd left off before her son's shortsword caught her attention. "What I was going to say is that we can't go back to Ostaville. They came for Yorlumin once and they'll come for him again."

"You're right. We can't go back," Yorlumin agreed to his wife, then turned to Rhys. "We'll accompany you to Krasnia. It's the least we can do. Not only did you risk your lives to save me and the other political prisoners, you took care of my children. I am forever indebted to you and your friends for your courage, kindness, and valor. As long as it's alright with-"

Yorlumin – along with everyone else – glanced at Kae. Before he'd even finished his sentence, she nodded and smiled.

"Then I guess just about all of us are going to Krasnia," Rhys said. "Assuming it stops snowing eventually."

The only ones in the cabin *not* going to Krasnia were the three other former prisoners besides Ena and Yorlumin. Though well-aware of the risk involved in returning to Ostaville, all their belongings were there as well as their families. But no one would be going anywhere for the remainder of the day. Every time someone checked outside, it was still snowing heavily. Even after dark the snow continued to fall, though it seemed to be gradually letting up.

16.

The next morning, everyone was pleased to see it had stopped snowing overnight. There wasn't a cloud in the sky and as soon as the sun came up over the horizon, the snow gradually started melting. Eager to get moving, everyone ate a quick breakfast, packed their belongings, and headed out the door. The three former prisoners going back to Ostaville thanked the others and began traveling north on foot toward the town. Those who remained headed south toward Seenia with the three horses. This time, they didn't go over the Seenia Mountains like they had on the way up. With over a foot of slushy snow accumulated on the ground, it would've been hard to climb up the side of the mountain. And even without any snow, the horses wouldn't have been able to make it up them.

The fairly large group – twelve in all, including the two children – took the road going around the eastern side of the mountains. During that first day, they noticed less and less snow on the ground the farther south they traveled. By the time they stopped for the night, there was no snow on the ground at all.

The next two days of travel went by uneventfully. They passed adventurers and merchants along the way, but didn't stop to talk to any of them. With Sandor, Malaric, and the two kids – the slowest members of the group – riding on the horses, they made really good time and got to the outskirts of Seenia on that third evening.

"After helping Larnyk kill those guards," Wynn said, "I probably shouldn't go into Seenia."

"And since the reason you and Larnyk killed those guards was because they were after *me*," Sandor added, "*I* should probably stay out of Seenia, too."

"I think it's best if as few people go into town as necessary," Rhys said. Everyone agreed. "Why don't we set up camp near Zeleny Pond just east of Seenia. A few people can run into town to grab some food for the rest of us while we do."

A Seenia native, Ena offered to go into town. Yorlumin and his daughter asked to go with her and she agreed.

"I'd also like to go," Nyvernia, the half-elven Rising Shadow member said. "I have a friend in Seenia I'd like to visit. I'll keep it brief."

"Is your friend someone who's sympathetic to our cause?" Braylin asked Nyvernia. "Do you want me to go with you?"

Nyvernia said no to both. After finding a good spot away from the road near Zeleny Pond to spend the night, Ena, Yorlumin, Farryn, and Nyvernia walked into town. Ena wore her hood, but the others had no reason to hide their identities.

"I'll meet you back at the campsite," Nyvernia said as they got to a fork in the road.

"Okay," Ena replied.

As Nyvernia headed left at the fork, the others went right to go get food and drinks to bring back to camp. They passed what little remained of Obscene, Larnyk's beloved tavern, along the way. In front of the ruins, a new sign had been put up. In Common it read: *Closed during renovation. Under new management. Coming soon: Scenic – a weapons-and-magic-free tavern for races of all ages!* Seeing the burned-down tavern and the sign out front made Malaric and Ena sad.

They continued up the road until they got to The Scene. The place was even more packed than it had been the last time they were there. Aside from a couple empty stools at the bar, there was nowhere to sit. Not a single table was open. Fortunately, they didn't plan to stay: they were only picking up stuff to bring back to camp. Malaric noticed Calum and the other halflings sitting at the same table they'd been at when he met them a couple weeks earlier. While Ena ordered the food and drinks to go, Malaric wandered over to their table.

"Excuse me. I don't know if you remember me but-"

"Malaric, right?" Calum asked.

"That's right! How did you-"

"I'm psychic," Calum replied with a straight face. Malaric's eyebrows lowered. Then Calum burst out in laughter and said, "I'm kidding, I'm kidding. Just a little halfling humor. You've got the same expensive bag of healing supplies, for one," Calum said, first pointing to the bag, then to a pouch on Malaric's hip. "But *that's* the real giveaway right there. I can see you're on HRT. You might want to keep your herbs for racial transitioning in the bag with your medicinal herbs, especially if you're heading south. If people down in Krasnia see you carrying them around, they might give you a bit of trouble. Not everyone is as open minded down there."

"Don't I know it," Malaric replied, moving the pouch from his hip to his bag. "Thanks for the advice."

"So," Calum asked, "how do you like being a halfling so far? Is it everything you'd hoped it would be?"

"I'm still getting used to it, to be honest. But overall I'm glad I did it."

"Has your rude human friend been giving you a hard time?" one of the other halflings asked.

"He did at first," Malaric replied. "But surprisingly, he actually apologized for all the times he made fun of me. It was a nice moment."

"Even *I'm* surprised," Calum said. "That guy seemed like the type to never apologize for anything."

"Mal!" Ena yelled from across the tavern. "All set. Time to go!"

Malaric said goodbye to the halflings and rejoined Ena, Yorlumin, and Farryn. They'd ordered several jugs of wine and ale, a couple baskets of mutton, and four loaves of bread. Each of them grabbed as much as they could carry and left The Scene. As they were walking back through Seenia on their way to Zeleny Pond, the group noticed Nyvernia coming out of a house off in the distance. They weren't close enough to hear anything, but could see Nyvernia shaking hands with a dwarf outside the door. All of them stopped in the middle of the road.

"I know that house," Ena said. "It's the home of one of Seenia's top guards."

"Stay here, stay low, and stay quiet," Malaric replied and put down the big jug of ale he'd been carrying – or trying to. The jug was almost as tall as the halfling.

"Where are you going?" Ena asked.

"I'm going to use my stealth skill to get a little closer. See if I can hear anything."

Malaric crept along the road staying low, then disappeared into someone's yard. He managed to get close enough to Nyvernia and the dwarf to hear their conversation.

"I can't thank you enough for coming to me," the dwarf said. "I'm going to assemble a group of guards to go raid the rebel camp at Zeleny Pond right away. If all goes well, Duke Tolkatel will undoubtedly make me a knight. I might even get to meet the king and queen."

"Just make sure it doesn't look like I tipped you off," Nyvernia replied.

"Don't worry. It won't. And I'll make sure you get captured, not killed."

"And remember: there are two children with the group."

"We'll do our best not to kill them, either," the dwarf said. "Again, thank you, Nyvernia. Now if you'll excuse me, I have to put on my gear and get moving."

"Ahem," Nyvernia said and held out her hand.

"Of course," the dwarf replied, disappearing into the house for a moment. He returned to the door and placed a few platinum pieces in Nyvernia's hand. "There you go. I think that's fair."

"Most fair," Nyvernia agreed. "I have to get back to camp. Don't forget to make sure your guards know not to attack me."

The dwarf nodded, then disappeared into his house once again, this time closing the door. Nyvernia glanced over each of her shoulders. Satisfied no one was watching her, she walked to the road and began heading back to Zeleny Pond. Malaric stealthily rushed back to Ena, Yorlumin, and Farryn to tell them everything he'd overheard.

"We have to get back to warn the others," Ena said and everyone agreed.

Carrying the food and drinks, they hurried up the road. Ena stopped when she realized Malaric had fallen far behind the others, even behind Farryn who was practically running to keep up. She turned around to see the halfling waddling up the road, unable to see where he was going with the large jug of ale in his hands.

"Leave it," Ena said to Malaric. "Leave the ale."

"Wynn and I finally make peace after a lifetime of conflict and you want me to leave behind the thing he's looking forward to the most?" Malaric replied.

"If he's not alive to drink the ale, it won't matter, will it?" Yorlumin asked, rhetorically.

Malaric agreed with Ena and Yorlumin, and put the jug down on the side of the road. He took out his waterskin and, after emptying out all the water, filled it with as much ale as it would hold. Then they continued up the road, all of them walking quickly. Along the way, they agreed not to tell the others about Nyvernia's involvement – not yet. Before long, they got back to the campsite at Zeleny Pond. Nyvernia was already there standing next to Braylin.

"Where's the ale?" Wynn asked the second they got back.

"I left it on the side of the road," Malaric replied.

"You did *what*?" Wynn shouted. "Why in the name of Xamos would you do such a thing?"

"Because we needed to get back here as quickly as possible and it was too heavy," Ena replied. "Seenia's guards know we're here. We have to leave right now."

"How do *you* know *they* know we're here?" Braylin asked.

Nyvernia took a step away from Braylin, who didn't seem to notice.

"We overheard two guards talking as they hurried down Seenia's main road," Malaric answered.

Nyvernia stepped back over to Braylin. Malaric could see the relief in Nyvernia's face when he said it was two guards they'd overheard and not her.

"How could the guards possibly know we're here?" Braylin asked.

*Clip, clop. Clip, clop. Clip, clop.*

"I don't know," Rhys replied when they heard horses off in the distance. "But we've got to move. Now!"

Everyone gathered their stuff as quickly as possible and started heading south. Though the sun had set, one three-quarters-full moon was directly overhead with the other coming up over the horizon. The moons provided just enough light to see where they were going without having to light torches or cast an illumination spell. The group followed along the edge of Zeleny Pond until they got to its southernmost point where the Zeleny Mountains began.

*Clip, clop. Clip, clop. Clip, clop.*

The sound of horses was no longer far off in the distance: they were getting closer – much closer. Though the group didn't want to abandon their own three horses, they knew their only chance of getting away would be by going up into the mountains on foot. After all, this wasn't the first time they'd found themselves in such a situation. Ayen, Farryn, and Sandor got down from the horses.

"Off you go," Wynn said, giving one of the horses a slap on its backside. "Ya!"

The horse bolted off into the night and the other two followed right behind it. As the sound of their hooves got softer, the sound of the guards' horses got louder. The closer they got, the more of them the group could tell there were.

"Do any of you see a way up the mountain?" Rhys asked.

Everyone spread out along its edge to look for a way up. The rocky terrain was largely impassible.

"Look Mom," Farryn said, pulling on her mother's chainmail shirt with one hand and pointing to a narrow trail leading up the mountain with the other.

"Here," Kae half-yelled. "We found a path!"

Everyone rushed over to Farryn and Kae. With the horses closing in on them, they all headed up the mountain. The trail was so narrow they had to walk single-file. In some spots it was barely passable, but they managed to continue onward. Just a few minutes later, they heard the horses – a dozen, at least – get to the bottom of Zeleny Pond. The horses stopped and they heard voices, but couldn't make out what was being said. Everyone stayed perfectly still, trying to be as quiet as possible. A moment later, the horses galloped off heading east along the southern edge of Zeleny Pond. But they could still hear the faint sound of movement coming from the bottom of the mountain.

"Sounds like most of them are gone," Braylin whispered. "They must've seen our horses' hoof prints and thought we'd continued around the pond. But they might've sent a guard or two up this trail to make sure we didn't go up it."

"What are you doing?" Rhys whispered to Wynn, who'd positioned himself behind a large boulder.

"Ugh!" Wynn groaned as he tried to push it down the mountain. It didn't budge. "I'm trying to make sure that, if they did send guards up the trail after us, they'll get stuck. You just going to stand there or are ya going to help me?"

Rhys joined Wynn behind the massive rock. They both pushed it as hard as they could. The boulder finally came loose and tumbled down the mountain. It crashed into several other rocks along the way, dislodging some and shattering others. Though they couldn't see very far down the path, everyone agreed it was no longer passable: the trail had barely been passable to begin with. Confident they couldn't be followed, the group continued up the mountain.

After about an hour, they decided to stop for the night. The sound of horses was long gone, as was the sound of movement coming from below. Yorlumin found a cave large enough for all of them to sleep in and they set up camp around it.

Malaric waited for an opportunity to talk to Rhys discreetly. Once everyone was settled into camp, he found one. The two of them talked privately for a few minutes. None of the others, Nyvernia included, seemed to notice. They were all too busy eating and drinking around the campfire. Malaric told Rhys everything he'd witnessed and overheard in Seenia. After thinking about it for a minute, Rhys suggested they tell Braylin and Malaric agreed.

"I think we're safe up here," Rhys said, addressing everyone a few minutes later. "But we still need to be vigilant all night. Braylin, will you take first watch?"

She nodded.

"I'll take second," Rhys continued. "Wynn, will you take third?"

With a mouthful of mutton, he nodded. Kae and Iolas agreed to take the last two watches. Malaric walked over to Wynn and sat down next to him. The halfling took out his waterskin, took a sip, and offered it to Wynn.

"I know it isn't much," Malaric said. "But it's all I could carry."

Wynn nodded, took a swig, and handed it back.

"What? You're not going to comment on how I could've carried more if I was still human or something like that?"

"You almost sound like you *want* me to make fun of you."

"Definitely not. I'm just not used to you *not* making fun of me. What changed?"

"You did," Wynn said, taking another swig of ale as they passed the waterskin back and forth. "I always thought you were full of shit. But actually seeing you as a halfling, knowing you felt strongly enough to actually go through with the transformation-"

"Transition," Malaric corrected.

"Whatever," Wynn continued. "I never thought you'd actually go through with it. Now that you have, I kind of feel like a dick for making fun of you so much. Hey, speaking of dicks..."

With the waterskin in hand, Wynn pointed at Malaric's crotch.

"Yes," Malaric replied. "I'm *fully* halfling."

"Can I-"

"No," Malaric interrupted, knowing exactly what Wynn was going to ask. "You can't see it."

"Hey, I've got an idea. I wonder if I could have a wizard leave the rest of my body alone but transition just my junk – not that I'm unhappy with what I've got now. But how beast would I be if I was still my normal human self but with a big, scaly dragon dick? Wouldn't that be awesome? Think I could convince a wizard that my human dick identifies as a dragon's?"

"If anyone could do it, you could," Malaric replied. They both laughed.

The two of them continued passing the waterskin back and forth until they finished the ale. After a long day of traveling, everyone was tired and soon laid down to go to sleep – everyone but Braylin who had first watch. Malaric laid down with the rest of them, but only pretended to be sleeping. He stayed awake waiting for Nyvernia to drift off. When Malaric heard her snoring a while later, he quietly got up and walked over to Braylin.

"I have something important to tell you," Malaric whispered.

He told Braylin everything he'd seen and heard in Seenia. Even in the moonlight, Malaric could see her face turn red with anger.

"Part of me wants to slit that traitor's throat while she sleeps," Braylin whispered. "But knowing she's working for the crown could come in handy."

"Maybe it will," Malaric agreed. "Think about it and discuss it with Rhys when you wake him up for second watch. He wants to talk to you about what I told you, too, but thought it'd be best if you heard it from me since I'm the one who witnessed it."

"Thank you," Braylin replied. "You did the right thing by not calling Nyvernia out in front of everyone. We might be able to use this to our advantage – somehow."

Malaric could see the wheels turning inside Braylin's head. He left her alone, returning to his spot just as quietly as he'd gotten up. Before long, the halfling was out cold along with the others.

17.

After five days of uneventful travel over the mountains and through the Zeleny Forest, the group was getting close to Krasnia as the sun neared the horizon. Though only an hour-or-so from the town, they decided to spend one more night in the Zeleny Forest.

The next morning, everyone got up and prepared to head into Krasnia. Once the group was ready, Rhys and Braylin gathered everyone in a circle. The two of them had been secretly plotting for days.

"I've got some very exciting news," Braylin said, "especially for my fellow Rising Shadow members. After everything that happened in Ostaville, our group has recruited dozens of new members – many of whom are skilled adventurers – to come down to Krasnia to confront the king and queen with us. They left Ostaville right behind us and will arrive in Krasnia by day's end. So we need to lay low until they arrive and then we'll all make our move together."

"Malaric," Rhys said, "since your house is the farthest from both the royal castle and the center of town, we've chosen there to wait for them to arrive – if that's alright with you."

Malaric nodded.

"How do you know all this?" Nyvernia asked.

"A messenger came to me the other night," Braylin answered.

"What messenger?" Nyvernia asked. "How did they know where to find you?"

"Do you doubt me?" Braylin replied.

"Of course not. I just-"

"A magic-using scout with two bloodhounds, if you must know," Braylin said. "Even with the dogs and the magic, he said it wasn't easy to find me. But obviously he did."

"So we're just going to wait at Malaric's house until they arrive?" Nyvernia asked.

"We can't risk being recognized, so yes – mostly. A couple of us will be able to leave Malaric's house, but only those who no one around town will recognize."

"Even though I've lived in Krasnia my entire life," Malaric said, "now with my new halfling body, I'm one of those people."

"No one knows *me* in Krasnia. You should have me go out, too," Nyvernia suggested.

"Excellent idea," Braylin replied and put a hand on her shoulder. "I can always count on you, Nyvernia."

They all walked to Malaric's house being careful not to attract any attention along the way. It wasn't a very large house, but it was big enough for everyone to find a spot in the living room to get comfortable while they talked.

"The scout who visited the other night told me their party's less than a half-day away from ours," Braylin said. "They'll be coming down the main road. Since they don't know where Malaric's house is, we'll need someone to wait for them along the road. We could also use someone to go around Krasnia talking to the townsfolk to make sure no one knows they're coming. We obviously have a traitor in our organization somewhere."

Nyvernia took a deep breath. Even though Braylin made sure it didn't look like she'd noticed, she did.

"But I know it isn't anyone in this room," Braylin continued. Nyvernia exhaled. "Malaric and Nyvernia – one of you needs to wait along the northern road and the other needs to go around town talking to people. I'll let you two decide who does what."

"Even though I look different now," Malaric said to Nyvernia, "lots of people in Krasnia know me. It's possible someone might figure out who I am if I go around talking to people. So I should probably be the one to wait north of town if that's alright with you."

"I was going to suggest the very same thing," she replied and smiled.

"Excellent," Braylin said. "Since we don't know exactly when they'll get into town, you two should get going soon."

Malaric and Nyvernia loaded up their gear, getting ready to go. Once they were all set, the two of them headed for the door. On their way out, Rhys whispered to Malaric, making sure Nyvernia couldn't hear him.

"Keep a close eye on her, but don't let her see you. And be careful."

Rhys shut the door, then watched Nyvernia and Malaric disappear down the road through a window. Once they were out of sight, Rhys clapped his hands and addressed the group.

"Okay, it's time to move! If Nyvernia goes where we think she's going, it won't be long until this house is crawling with knights, guards, and maybe even a few off-duty night guards."

While everyone hurriedly gathered their gear, Yorlumin said to his wife, "One of us should stay somewhere safe with the kids."

"Awww," Ayen protested. "I want to go!"

"You'll get your chance to go on plenty of adventures – but not this one," Kae replied to her son, then turned to Yorlumin. "And since I got to go on the last adventure, I suppose you want me to stay with the kids?"

"That's our agreement – one for you, one for me. Take them and get a room at the inn."

Kae nodded to her husband. Rhys came out of Malaric's bedroom carrying several hooded robes, none of which would've fit the human-turned-halfling anymore. He handed one to Wynn and one to Ena, then put a robe on himself.

"Make sure your faces are fully hidden," Rhys said to them. "We can't risk anyone recognizing us."

Once everyone was ready, they all left Malaric's house. Kae took the two kids and, following Rhys' directions, headed to the inn. The others traveled around the edge of Krasnia to the eastern side of town where the royal castle was located. When they got there, all of them hid in the woods directly across from the drawbridge – the royal castle's only entrance and exit. It was lowered, as the drawbridge usually was during the day.

Nothing happened for a while. They patiently waited, keeping a close eye on the drawbridge. Then Malaric showed up, startling the group.

"Did Nyvernia do what I thought she would?" Braylin asked.

"Yup," Malaric replied. "She headed straight for the royal castle just like you said."

"Then it's just a matter of time until-"

Braylin stopped talking when they saw over a dozen knights on horseback and dozens of guards on foot flood out of the castle. They were all heavily armed and rushed over the drawbridge, up the road into Krasnia. Being careful to stay hidden while they watched the knights and guards rush out of the castle, the group waited until they were sure no more would be coming. Then, once the ones who did come out were down the road and out of sight, they came out of the woods and ran over the drawbridge.

Two guards stood outside the castle entrance. As soon as they saw everyone coming toward them, they ran inside and started pulling up the drawbridge. Malaric and Wynn were the first ones out of the woods and the only two to get across the drawbridge before it was too high to cross. They attacked the two guards while the others were stuck on the other side of the moat.

Unable to see what was happening, Rhys and the others waited anxiously. Aside from the faint sound of metal on metal and an occasional grunt, they weren't able to hear much either. After what felt like an hour but was no more than a minute or two, the drawbridge lowered. Rhys and the others rushed over it, happy to see that Wynn and Malaric had come out victorious. They each had a few minor cuts but were otherwise fine.

"You know," Wynn said to Malaric, "you and I don't make a half-bad team. It was awesome how you jabbed one of your daggers into that guard's neck."

"You saw that?" Malaric replied. "Thanks. It was pretty awesome how *you* caved in that guard's face with a single blow – but you're always caving in faces."

Proudly, Wynn smiled.

"I love seeing the two of you bond, but we've got work to do," Rhys said, going over to the ropes used to raise and lower the drawbridge. "Wynn, help me out. We just watched almost all the royal knights and guards rush out of here and can't have them come rushing back in while we're still inside."

Raising the drawbridge took a lot more effort than lowering it. The two friends had to use all their strength to pull on the ropes. Slowly, the drawbridge raised until it was all the way up.

Rhys pulled out his longsword, pointed it up the red carpet, and said, "Now to go pay a little visit to the king and queen."

18.

The group worked their way through the castle to the throne room. Rhys, Wynn, Ena, and Malaric noticed there were just as many servants around as the first time they'd visited the castle, but not guards. All the doorways – other than the main entrance – were left unguarded, making it easy to move through the castle quickly. As soon as any servants saw them storming through the castle, they scattered.

They knew they'd be approaching the throne room soon. Although there were no guards posted outside any of the doors they'd come through, they suspected the doorway to the throne room might be different. Malaric used his stealth skill to sneak up ahead while the others stayed put. Sure enough, two sentries were posted outside the large throne-room doors. The halfling crept back to the group to let everyone know and they all continued onward.

Ena and Braylin both started casting spells from around the corner of the hallway leading to the throne room. As they neared the end of the spells, they came out from around the corner and pointed at the two guards. The surprised sentries raised their weapons as soon as they noticed. A thin, fast-moving cloud of grey smoke shot from Braylin's fingertip at one guard, then from Ena's at the other. Two direct hits turned both guards into stone statues.

"You're going to kill them?" Rhys asked Wynn as he raised his warhammer and approached the statues. "They already can't move. The poor guys are just doing their job."

"And what do you suppose they're going to do when the spell wears off?" Wynn replied.

"Wynn's right," Malaric said.

After thinking it over for a moment, Rhys agreed. He didn't want anyone killed who didn't have to be, but knew the guards would come after them the first chance they got. Rhys nodded to Wynn, who nodded back. Then Wynn took his warhammer and turned both guards into a million pieces of rubble.

*Smash! Smash!*

As soon as the guards had been destroyed, everyone rushed over to the large throne-room doors. Rhys and Wynn used all their might to pry them open and the group stormed in. At the far end of the room, the king and queen sat in their thrones. Kneeling before them was Nyvernia.

"Guards!" the king shouted, pointing at the group. "Seize them!"

"Kill them!" the queen yelled, just a little louder than her husband.

Four lightly armored guards rushed over. There were at least twice as many servants in the room who all rushed *away* from the group. The guards raised their weapons – three longswords and a battleaxe – and attacked.

Rhys and Wynn made short work of the guards – with a little help from their friends. The two fighters stood in front, exchanging blows with the guards. From behind them, Iolas and Malaric used their ranged weapons to attack – a bow and throwing dagger, respectively. And behind them, Braylin, Yorlumin, and Ena started casting spells. But the fight was over before any of them finished.

Iolas launched an arrow at one of the guards.

The razor-sharp tip sliced right through the guard's neck. One down. Though it'd been some time since Malaric threw a dagger in combat, he launched one at a guard and it found its target. If the guard's left pupil was a bullseye, the throw was a perfect one. The tip landed dead-center in the guard's eye, piercing deep into the man's skull. Two down. Guard number three joined the ones on the flood when Wynn's warhammer caved in half his face. Three down. Rhys was the only one who didn't get a one-shot kill. It took him *two* swings to take out the forth guard.

"Is that all ya got?" Wynn asked and laughed.

"No, it's not," the queen replied matter-of-factly. Then she yelled, "Knights! Xuharis! Come at once!"

Four knights in full-plate armor and a wizard wearing one of the most elaborately decorated robes any of them had ever seen came out of a door to the left of the thrones. The wizard stayed safely behind the knights.

"Seize them!" the queen shouted, pointing at the group. "Kill them! Just get rid of them!"

From the back, Ena, Braylin, and Yorlumin each started casting another spell. Knowing his ranged weapon was of no use against knights wearing full-plate armor and with no clear shot at the wizard, Iolas dropped the bow in favor of his shortsword. Malaric retrieved his dagger from the guard's face and pulled out his other one.

For the next several minutes, the sound of metal on metal echoed around the room. The king and queen eagerly watched the action from the comfort of their thrones while Nyvernia watched from the discomfort of her knees. Around the edges of the room servants stood nervously – the ones who weren't able to take cover behind a pillar or statue – just as unable to peel their eyes away from the battle as everyone else.

Ena, Yorlumin, and Braylin each came to the ends of their spells. Had they coordinated their magic, they might've been able to end the fight right then and there. But each of them cast a different spell on a different knight. Ena used the same fire-magic spell that'd landed her in the dungeon of Ostaville's castle. Fireball after fireball launched from her fingertip at one of the knights. Ena was happy to see that, this time, her finger didn't turn red. A couple fireballs ricocheted off the knight's full-plate armor, one of which hit a tapestry on the far wall and it went up in flames. But several fireballs got under his armor, igniting the knight's hair and flesh.

"Arrrggghhh!" the knight screamed as he fell to the floor.

Yorlumin went with a spell he'd just cast a few minutes earlier – the same turn-to-stone spell that'd worked so well on the guards outside the throne room. And it worked just as well on the knights inside. Yorlumin turned the knight closest to Wynn into a statue knowing he'd destroy him with his warhammer. And that's exactly what Wynn did.

*Smash!*

The stone knight shattered. Braylin's spell was a little more creative and a lot more advanced. The floor below one of the two remaining knights started trembling. It shook so violently that he nearly toppled over. Then the ground opened up and swallowed the knight. As soon as he fell into the hole, it closed back up and the floor returned to normal.

With only one knight remaining in front of him, Xuharis appeared to finish whatever spell he'd been casting. Nothing seemed to happen. Then the wizard immediately started casting something else.

Wynn, Rhys, and Iolas attacked the last remaining knight. Knowing his daggers weren't going to do much damage against someone so heavily armored, Malaric backed off. Ena, Braylin, and Yorlumin all began casting another spell.

Though the knight was too busy trying to block his three attackers to do much attacking of his own, his efforts weren't in vain. The knight did an admirable job defending. None of them landed any significant blows against him. But when Braylin finished her spell, there was nothing the knight could do to defend against it.

*Zap!*

A single bolt of lightening ripped through the ceiling, hitting the top of the knight's helmet like a lightening rod. He immediately toppled over, smoke coming off his smoldering corpse.

The only enemy remaining was Xuharis. He looked like he was nearing the end of his second spell, but Yorlumin finished his first. Taking aim at the wizard, Yorlumin fired close to a dozen fireballs from his fingertip. Every one of them were right on target. But just an inch in front of the wizard, each fireball bounced off an invisible barrier and went flying right back in Yorlumin's direction. More than half of them hit Yorlumin and several hit Iolas who stood almost directly in between the two wizards.

"Ahhhggghhhggg!" Yorlumin screamed, running around in circles.

Unfortunately, he couldn't outrun the flames. Yorlumin collapsed to the floor and thrashed around violently. His final thought was that, though the spell Xuharis had cast *seemed* to have done nothing, it very much did. Yorlumin realized it was some sort of powerful magical shield or magic-reversal spell. Overwhelmed with burning pain and unable to breath with his body engulfed in flames, Yorlumin's eyes closed and his body stopped moving.

Though Iolas didn't get hit with nearly as many fireballs as Yorlumin, the end result was the same. The fireballs that did hit caused his entire body to go up in flames. But unlike Yorlumin who ran in circles screaming, Iolas stood perfectly still, perfectly silent until he dropped his shortsword and collapsed to the floor.

"Don't cast any more spells on the wizard!" Braylin shouted after piecing together what'd happened.

Xuharis was coming to the end of another spell. But before he could get out the last few words of the incantation, Malaric ran over to him and tried a move he'd never attempted: the double-*front*stab. The halfling leapt at the wizard trying to stab him in the neck and stomach. Malaric got it half right. One of his daggers plunged into the wizard's neck. But the other missed its mark by a few inches. Instead of hitting Xuharis' stomach, Malaric jabbed the dagger into his balls.

"Aggggggg," the wizard yelled – *tried to* yell.

Malaric's dagger sliced through Xuharis' vocal chords and blood poured from the wizard's neck. In a futile attempt to slow the bleeding, he clutched at it. But Xuharis' effort didn't make the slightest bit of difference. With one hand clutching his neck and the other his balls, the wizard collapsed to the floor.

"Is *that* all ya got?" Wynn asked the king and queen again, breathing heavily.

Rhys and Ena both shot him the evil eye. The king glanced at the queen, but she didn't look back at him.

"As a matter of fact," the king replied, "yes. I believe it is."

The survivors approached the king, queen, and Nyvernia. Several of them had to step over a dead knight or around one of their still-burning-ally's corpse. As Braylin approached Nyvernia, she picked up Iolas' shortsword from the floor.

"What are you doing here?" Nyvernia asked, her voice shaky. "I thought-"

"You thought what?" Braylin interrupted. "You thought we'd all be at Malaric's house waiting to get captured by the small army you sent after us?"

"Braylin, please," Nyvernia begged, still kneeling. "Let me explain."

"No," Braylin replied, standing over her. "Let *me* explain. You sought me out knowing I was one of Rising Shadow's founders. You pretended to believe in our cause, saying all the things you knew I wanted to hear. You earned not just my trust, but the trust of Sandor and the rest of Rising Shadow. Yet the whole time you were working for the crown. And for what, a few gold pieces? I don't know if I'm more angry or disgusted. Actually, more than anything, I'm disappointed. But not in you – in myself for trusting you. I should've known you were an infiltrator from the very beginning. If Malaric hadn't told me you were a spy back at Zeleny Pond, I still probably wouldn't know."

"You've known for that long?" Nyvernia asked, clearly surprised. "I don't know what Malaric told you but-"

"Silence!" Braylin shouted. Nyvernia stopped talking. Wrapping her fingers tightly around the hilt of Iolas' shortsword, Braylin calmly continued, "You're the worst kind of person, Nyvernia. You betrayed me and you betrayed Rising Shadow. For that, you shall pay the ultimate price. This is for Iolas and Yorlumin, who both might still be alive if it wasn't for you."

Braylin raised the shortsword high overhead. Nyvernia cowered, holding her hands up in front of her face.

"Please," she begged. "You don't have to do this."

Braylin swung the shortsword as hard as she could at Nyvernia's neck. In the hands of an experienced fighter, the sword could've easily decapitated her. But Braylin was a wizard and had never swung a sword in her entire life. The razor-sharp blade of Iolas' shortsword hit Nyvernia's neck, but only cut about one-third of the way through.

"Agggggg agggggg," Nyvernia croaked, clutching at her neck, blood pouring from both it and her mouth.

"Sorry!" Braylin exclaimed. "I didn't mean for you to suffer. I thought the sword would've gone right through. So sorry! Maybe if I..."

Braylin raised the shortsword once again. But before she had the chance to swing it, Nyvernia fell forward faceplanting between the king's feet and the queen's. Braylin dropped the bloody shortsword and stepped back. Blood continued to pour out of Nyvernia's neck, forming a pool around her lifeless body. The queen crossed her legs to avoid getting blood on her foot.

"*You*," Rhys said and stepped forward, pointing his longsword first at the king and then at the queen. "*And you*. This is all *your* doing."

"I don't know what you're talking about," the king replied.

"Snow. The MAKs up north. ANTIMA. Social judgment wizards. *You're* behind *all* of it! You're supposed to protect the people of Ravnia, not exploit them for your own selfish desires. We put our trust in you!"

"You don't know what you're talking about," the queen said, crossing her arms to match her legs.

"Rhys knows *exactly* what he's talking about," Sandor replied. "You pit the good people of Ravnia against one another over trivial nonsense, creating division where none need exist. White magic, black magic – it's all just magic! And it belongs in the hands of the people. But you want it all for yourself – you and the other oligarchs who rule this beautiful continent. That's why it was *you* behind the fire-magic ban and *you* who created snow so you can ban ice-and-maybe-even-all-water magic next. Then what, wind magic? Healing magic?"

"And it was *you* who sent *us* on a fool's errand," Rhys said. "You sent us to investigate snow when it was you and the other ogilarks-"

"Oligarchs," Sandor corrected.

"You and the other oligarchs," Rhys continued, "who'd ordered powerful wizards to created it. You used us from the very beginning!"

Neither the king nor queen replied. They both just sat there looking at Rhys and the others with contempt.

"And you can't even admit it," Ena said. "I bet neither of you feel even the slightest bit of remorse."

"The only thing I'm sorry for is sending *you* on this quest," the king replied.

"My whole life, I believed in you," Rhys said, stepping over Nyvernia's corpse to get closer to the king. "I trusted that the crown had our best interests at heart. But the only things you care about are platinum, pearls, and power. The people of Krasnia and the entire continent of Ravnia would be better off without such selfish rulers. They deserve better. *We* deserve better. And *you* deserve *this*."

Rhys' heart beat faster than the flapping of a

hummingbird's wings. Sweat dripped from his forehead and tears formed in the corners of his eyes. Still, Rhys didn't even blink, his eyes focused on the king. In a single motion, Rhys raised his longsword overhead and swung it.

*Swish!*

Thud!

With a single slice, Rhys chopped the king's head clean off. It thumped to the floor next to him. The queen watched with terror-filled, pupil-dilated eyes but didn't say a word. The king's headless body slumped to the side, blood flowing from the neck all over his finely stitched clothing and jewel-encrusted throne. For a moment the king's hands and feet twitched, his scepter falling to the floor. Gradually, the blood flow slowed.

The servants around the edge of the room watched in horror – mostly. But as terrified as they all were, a few of them couldn't stop the corners of their mouths from rising. The king could be quite cruel to some of them – most of them, really – and were happy to see him get what they believed he deserved.

Rhys stood in front of the king's throne until the headless body stopped twitching. Then he turned to the queen.

"It was all *his* idea," she said, pointing to her deceased husband. The queen spoke faster than usual and her pointer finger trembled – as did the rest of her body. "He's the king. I'm just the queen. I didn't have anything to do with-"

*Crunch!*

"Equality," Wynn said after caving in the queen's face with his warhammer. He kissed the head of his weapon, getting some of the queen's blood on his lips, then added, "I think I'll name you The Equalizer."

*Ching, cling.*

Rhys dropped his longsword and fell to his knees. Aside from the sound of the sword hitting the floor, the large room was completely silent and stayed that way for a while.

19.

Wynn walked over to the king. He grabbed an arm, yanked the corpse off the throne, picked up the scepter, sat down, and put his feet up on the king's headless body.

"Look at me," Wynn said with a big, goofy grin on his face, scepter in hand. "I'm the king!"

Several servants who'd been hiding behind statues and pillars came out now that the violence had seemed to stop. They began chatting with other servants – the ones who'd been along the wall and saw everything – to get all the gory details.

The group gathered together directly in front of the thrones. Malaric checked Iolas-and-Yorlumin's still-smoldering bodies to see if he could heal either of them, then joined the others. Braylin looked at him with a glimmer of hope in her eyes. When Malaric shook his head side to side, Braylin's eyebrows lowered and that hope vanished.

"I can't believe it," Rhys said. "All of it. Everything I believed in, everyone I trusted – it was all a lie. I don't even know what to do."

"I have a suggestion," Sandor replied. "Something we *all* should do: get out of here. We just committed double-regicide. Eventually the royal knights and guards will return. And when they do, if we're still here-"

"Sandor's right," Ena said. "Some of us are in rough shape. We won't survive a major confrontation."

While listening to the others talk, Malaric noticed a few servants going through a door behind the king's throne to the right. No one else seemed to

notice them, nor did they notice when Malaric left the group and slipped through the door himself.
However, they *did* notice when he came out.

"Look what I found," Malaric said, holding up his arms.

His little halfling hands were filled with gems and platinum pieces. On Malaric's head was a jewel-encrusted tiara. He'd tried on two different crowns, but they were too big for his head and just slid to his shoulders.

Everyone in the group headed for the back door. Wynn was the first, enthusiastically hopping up from the king's throne. The dead ruler's decapitated head was directly in Wynn's path to the room and he booted it out of his way. Many more servants rushed through the doorway as well. Rhys was the last one to join the others. He picked up his longsword from the floor, sheathed it, and headed through the back door down a long hall. The first hallway door was to the king and queen's bedroom. There didn't seem to be anything of value in there – anything that could easily be carried out – other than some fine clothing and a few pieces of jewelry. Rhys continued down the hall until he got to the room with all the treasure.

The room was much smaller than the throne room. But it was large enough to contain piles of gems, jewelry, gold, platinum, and other valuables of unimaginable wealth. There was more than enough for all the servants and everyone in the group to take whatever they wanted.

"Grab as much as you can carry and let's get out of here," Rhys said.

Everyone filled their bags, pouches, and wherever else they could stuff a few gems or coins. Then they all headed out of the treasure room, down the hallway, and back to the throne room. While in there, a couple of them searched Nyvernia, Yorlumin, and Iolas' bodies, taking a few random items.

Just as Rhys had been the last of the group to enter the treasure room, he was the last to exit. Though he could've easily carried twice as many valuables, Rhys didn't want to be greedy. On his way out, he turned to the servant-filled room.

"Your turn," Rhys said to the servants. "There's more than enough for all of you. It makes me sick to my stomach to think all this wealth was just sitting here while there's so much poverty all over Ravnia. Royalty or not, no one should have so much while others have so little."

Rhys returned to the throne room to join the others. When he did, the remaining servants rushed through the back door toward the treasure room. The group heard cheers and screams of happiness coming from there, which almost made Rhys smile.

"In case I wasn't clear before, I'll say it again," Sandor said. "We have to get out of here *now*!"

The group left the throne room and followed the red carpet back to the castle's entrance. Rhys and Wynn lowered the drawbridge. Everyone rushed across it and headed into Krasnia.

"Someone needs to tell Kae what happened to her husband," Rhys said. "The kids, too. Ayen and Farryn deserve to know what happened to their father."

Half of the group looked from one person to the next. The other half didn't look at anything but the ground. Clearly, none of them wanted to be the bearer of bad news.

"I'll tell them," Wynn finally said when it became obvious none of the others were going to volunteer.

"Do it quickly," Rhys replied. "Then meet the rest of us at the tavern. Hurry!"

Wynn nodded, then rushed to the inn. Rhys and the others went straight to the tavern. When the bloody group walked through the door, the place immediately fell silent. Even though Rhys, Ena, and Malaric had all been to the tavern a million times before, none of the employees and only a couple patrons recognized them. It wasn't hard to understand why they didn't recognize Malaric – he was no longer human. But Rhys was still very much human and Ena was still an elf. However, between the expensive equipment the crown had given them and the fact they were covered in blood – some their own, some not – almost everyone in the tavern looked at them like they were strangers from a far-away land.

Rhys grabbed a chair from an unoccupied table and stood on it so everyone in the tavern could see him – and see him they did. All eyes were on Rhys. He took a deep breath, cleared his throat, and addressed the entire tavern.

"The king and queen are dead!" he proclaimed, pausing for a response.

Not a peep.

Not a single person cheered, booed, or even gasped. Sandor pulled another chair from the empty table. Braylin and Ena helped the old man get on it.

"For years," Sandor said, "they've taken more and more of your hard-earned gold. And in return you've gotten less and less. They've been taking away your freedoms one by one while increasing their own power. They've made you fearful and suspicious of others – even you own neighbors – pitting you against *each other* so you don't rise up against *them*. Today, their tyranny has come to an end. The king and queen are indeed dead."

Still, no one said a word. The patrons couldn't tell if this was a theatrical production by a group of traveling bards, some sort of strange joke, or what. But they soon realized these were no bards and it was no joke when Rhys, still standing on the chair, dug into his bag and pulled out two handfuls of platinum pieces. He threw them up in the air toward the middle of the tavern.

Instantly, the room went from being totally silent to erupting into chaos as everyone tried to snatch as many coins as they could. Every single butt in the tavern left its chair as patrons dove *over* tables, *under* tables, and in the case of one drunken half-elf, directly *into* the corner of a table. Several plates of food and mugs of ale ended up on the floor. The workers would've been furious had they noticed, but were all too busy trying to get their hands on some platinum for themselves. After most of it had been picked up, fights began breaking out between patrons.

"I saw it first!" a dwarven woman yelled, shoving a half-elven man.

"Well, I *grabbed* it first!" the man replied and pushed her back.

Fighting was the last thing Rhys wanted to happen. He clapped his hands together from atop the chair, but no one seemed to notice. When that didn't get anyone's attention, Braylin stuck two fingers in her mouth and whistled so loud it hurt the ears of anyone within a few feet of her. That *did* get the tavern's attention.

"No need to fight!" Rhys shouted. "There's a lot more where that came from. The royal castle is totally unguarded, drawbridge down. Once you get there, follow the red carpet to the throne room. Take the door behind the right throne and in the second door down the hallway, you'll see piles and piles of treasure. Go help yourself to as much platinum, gold, and other valuables as you can carry!"

Again, the tavern fell completely silent – but only for about half a second. Eyes darted around the room as if to see what the others were thinking. Then at the same time everyone – patrons and employees alike – rushed out the door and ran as fast as they could to the royal castle. Within seconds, the tavern was empty, aside from Rhys and the others. He got down from the chair and the group left the building.

Just as they were leaving the tavern, Wynn, Kae, and the two children arrived. Though Kae and Ayen seemed to have held it together when they heard the news about Yorlumin, it was obvious Farryn had been crying. The poor girl was still sniffling, doing everything she could to hold back another round of tears. But it wasn't enough. Again, Farryn began sobbing.

"Oh, I almost forgot," Wynn said and began digging through his bag. It took a minute to find what he was looking for because the bag was practically overflowing with coins and gems. When he found it, Wynn got down on one knee and handed Farryn a book. "I grabbed this for you. It's something to remember your father by."

She immediately stopped crying and wiped the tears from her eyes. Wynn had handed her Yorlumin's magic book, which she recognized right away. Farryn held the book to her chest, hugging it tightly. As sad as the girl was, the book still managed to put the slight hint of a smile on her face. Wynn got up and turned to Rhys.

"So, what now?" Wynn asked. "You proved snow is real. You found out the king and queen – along with several dukes and top CEOs – were conspiring against the people they're supposed to be protecting. And as if all that wasn't enough, you went ahead and killed the king and queen. Well, *you* killed the king. *I* killed the queen. But my point is, they're both dead. So I ask you: what now?"

"Now," Rhys replied, "we go after the other conspirators – those of us who choose to. But I wouldn't blame any of you if you decide to go your own way."

"Will there be skulls to smash?" Wynn asked.

"There will," Rhys replied. "Lots."

"Then I'm in," Wynn stated.

"I'm in," Ena added.

"Me too," Malaric said.

Braylin and Sandor both nodded to Rhys. He and the others looked at Kae.

"Can we help, Mom?" Ayen asked, pulling on Kae's arm. "Can we? Can we?"

"Dad would've wanted us to help," Farryn said, her arms still wrapped tightly around her father's magic book.

Kae nodded first to her daughter, then son, and finally to Rhys. He looked around the group, proud to be among such honorable adventurers. Rhys flashed the closest thing to a smile he could muster and nodded. Then his lips and neck straightened, all business.

"Let's get going," Rhys said. "There's still much to be done."

"Where to?" Ena asked. "We can't stick around Krasnia with the entire royal guard looking for us. And when they realize what we did to the king and queen, they'll be looking even harder."

"It wouldn't be wise to travel north to Seenia or Ostaville right now, either," Malaric added.

"Then I guess that only leaves us with one option," Rhys said. "We'll travel south to Yoog. There we can rest and figure out what our next move will be."

Everyone agreed. So the group headed south for the town of Yoog. Shortly after leaving Krasnia – though they were no longer there to see it themselves – a few snowflakes began falling from the sky.

## From The Author

Thank you for reading Snow. Of the fiction I've published so far, this book has been the funnest to write. Some of the ideas in Snow have been kicking around inside my head for a long time. It felt great to finally get them out. I hope you enjoyed reading Snow as much as I enjoyed writing it!

If you did like Snow, please take a moment to leave a review wherever you got it. And if you have any friends who might like Snow, please share it with them. From the top to the bottom of my heart, thank you!

## **Ellis Michaels Website**

ellismichaels.com

## **Follow Ellis on Social Media**

Facebook: @ellismichaelsauthor

Twitter: @ellismichaels9

Instagram: @ellismichaels9

TikTok: @ellis_michaels

## **Fiction by Ellis Michaels**

A Different Kind of Magic

Bad Unicorn

Ordinary Hero

The Bloodfeast Trilogy


## **Non-Fiction by Ellis Michaels**

Finding Happiness Through Pain and Embarrassment:
My Life With Behcet's Disease – A Memoir

## A Different Kind of Magic

### Pick a card, any card.

Eli has loved magic – the pick-a-card, any-card kind – for as long as he can remember. The talented young magician is forced to leave home and attend a private school in Salem, Massachusetts—the most notable location in the history of witchcraft. Once there, he's shocked to learn of the hand fate has dealt him. Magic – far greater than any parlor trick – lies within him, waiting to be unleashed.

But Eli isn't the only one eager to tap into that power.

His potential has caught the attention of another, one with sinister intentions and a cruel plan. Witches begin disappearing, with Eli's own father and sister as victims. What this has to do with him, Eli has yet to uncover.

Now, to prevent anyone else from getting hurt, Eli must learn to harness the magic within him... before his lurking enemy can claim it as their own.

*Fans of gripping urban fantasy and young adult page-turners are sure to love A Different Kind of Magic written by Ellis Michaels!*

***A Different Kind of Magic is available in both print and ebook formats.***

# Finding Happiness Through Pain & Embarrassment: My Life With Behcet's Disease – A Memoir

Can you imagine going to bed every night knowing you might wake up blind, deaf, paralyzed, or worse - not at all?

Ellis Michaels doesn't have to imagine it. He's been living it for decades. And so have thousands of others diagnosed with Behcet's disease.

Like Crohn's, Lupus, fibromyalgia, chronic fatigue syndrome, MS, and dozens of other illnesses, Behcet's is an autoimmune disease. Though each is unique, they all cause the body to attack itself. And Ellis's body has been kicking the crap out of him for decades. Here are just a few of the horrible symptoms he's experienced:

- Massive blood clots (DVTs) in both legs
- A clot in his inferior vena cava (vein going to the heart)
- Deep, open ulcers in his mouth
- Quarter-sized open sores on his... On the last place a guy would want them
- Severe eye inflammation leading to blindness that literally happened overnight
- Golf-ball-sized cysts on his face, neck, and ears

And that was all before Ellis had even turned 18.

Living with Behcet's disease (sometimes called Behcet's syndrome) can be an everyday struggle filled with pain and suffering. And while Ellis's journey has been a bumpy one to say the least, filled with depression, anxiety, drug addiction, and at times utter despair, he's managed to live an awesome life in spite of his diagnosis. By learning to see the silver linings of his illness, by focusing on the positives instead of the negatives, Ellis transformed his mind, his body, and his entire life. This is the story of how Ellis Michaels managed to find happiness through the pain and embarrassment of living with Behcet's disease.

*** *Warning! This memoir contains language and subject matter that might not be suitable for sensitive readers. There are discussions about drug use, mental illness, sex, suicide, and certain below-the-belt body parts. If you find these topics or occasional profanity distasteful, this book won't be your cup of tea. But Behcet's is a distasteful disease and can't be discussed in an open and honest manner without including these things.* ***

**Finding Happiness Through Pain and Embarrassment is available in print, ebook, and audiobook formats wherever books are sold.**